"Maybe I'm a v..., but I'm not go...

Tears glittered in Abbie's eyes. "And it's not the end of the world. My... fiancé and I'll have a place of our own one day. I'm not leaving this life forever."

A vice seemed to clamp on Yates's heart. She really had no chance of happiness, because she was right— she was made for a kind of life that was vanishing. What did she have left, except her blind faith in her no-good boyfriend?

And that faith was going to die. He himself would kill it. And he would lie to her up until the moment he did it. Well, it was his job, Yates rationalized. Hypocrisy for the sake of justice had become natural to him.

Merry Christmas, Abbie, he thought grimly as he wrestled the big, fragrant tree through the door. *Peace on earth and death to dreams.*

Dear Reader,

Nebraska and December have special meaning for me. My son, a fifth-generation Nebraskan, was born in Wayne County the day after Christmas.

On one side, his great-great-grandparents had come to Nebraska from Ireland. On the other side, they had come from Norway. Both sets were pioneers who made their living from the land.

My grandmother, aunt, uncles and father could tell stirring tales of life in rural Nebraska. Throughout all these stories ran a common theme: a love of the land and nature. No matter how harsh Nebraska could be, it could be strikingly beautiful, as well.

Once upon a time, the West was characterized by ranches, cowboys, pioneers and homesteaders. There was still land to be claimed, and the family farm and family ranch were common entities. But times change. Our age is dominated by the town, the city, the suburb. For many, the old order—and a treasured way of life—seems about to end.

Some people willingly give up this life, abandoning it for something new. Some are forced to give it up because of harsh economic realities. And some, stubbornly committed to the land they love, fight to preserve their rural heritage.

This is a story about all three kinds of people—the members of the Hale family—as they dispute the fate of SkyRim Ranch. It is also a story of love: love of land, love of family and romantic love.

So welcome to Christmas at SkyRim Ranch, my favorite season in my favorite state!

Sincerely,

Bethany Campbell

P.S. I love to hear from readers! You can write me at P.O. Box 6953, Springdale, Arkansas 72762.

THE MAN WHO CAME FOR CHRISTMAS
Bethany Campbell

Harlequin Books

TORONTO • NEW YORK • LONDON
AMSTERDAM • PARIS • SYDNEY • HAMBURG
STOCKHOLM • ATHENS • TOKYO • MILAN
MADRID • WARSAW • BUDAPEST • AUCKLAND

To the children of Victor Bostwick:
Bud, Dale, Jeannette, Bob, Betty, Marilyn,
Marge, Jerry, Emily and Larry

ISBN 0-373-03293-5

THE MAN WHO CAME FOR CHRISTMAS

Copyright © 1993 by Bethany Campbell.

CHAPTER ONE

THE WINDOWS of the sun porch were blind with December frost.

Abbie Hale knelt beside the heater, giving the foal his bottle. She had to hold the colt's head at the correct angle, or the formula would dribble down his jaws, matting his white coat.

She hadn't wanted to look at her father. All they'd done lately, it seemed, was quarrel. But now she stared up at him in disbelief.

"What?" was all she could say.

"The Connley man's coming—tonight," Frazier Hale kept his voice as obdurate as his expression. "I don't want any temperamental nonsense out of you. Make him feel at home."

Abbie's jaw tightened, her body stiffened. It was as if the winter cold had suddenly penetrated inside, chilling her heart's core.

"Why didn't you tell me sooner?" she demanded. She felt betrayed, ambushed. Christmas was turning out to be terrible enough without her father springing *this* surprise.

"Abbie, he's a busy man. He didn't know himself if he could make it until this morning. I know it's short notice. But when he comes, I want him made welcome," Frazier warned. "I mean it."

"You said the appraiser wouldn't come for a long time. You told me that again and again. If you want this . . . this

Connley person to feel welcome, keep him out of my way,'' Abbie said from between her teeth. "*I* don't want him here.''

"Abbie!'' Exasperation sharpened Frazier's tone.

"I mean it,'' she said, her voice flat with displeasure. "This is your idea, not mine. I don't want a stranger in the house, pawing through Grandpa's things. Especially at Christmas. It's . . . ghoulish.''

She was bone weary from caring for the colt, and her arms ached. She held the bottle up to the window's gray light. The formula, laced with antibiotics, was only half gone; the skeletal little foal was not an enthusiastic eater.

With a tired sigh, Abbie sat instead of knelt, propping the colt's head in her lap. The position wasn't as efficient, but she could hold the bottle in her right hand for a change. She used her left to stroke the animal's rough coat. She looked at his jutting ribs and shook her head in concern: he was so undersized, so thin, so sick. Yet this foal would live, she vowed. It *would.*

Out of the corner of her eye, she could see her father watching her. He was a large man, and the lines in his craggy face had been carved by fifty-nine years of scorching Nebraska summers and pitiless Nebraska winters.

Abbie, unlike her older brothers, did not resemble him in the slightest. She was small and blond and blue eyed, as her mother had been, with the same deceptive appearance of delicacy. She was emotional, too, as her mother had been, and she had the same love of the land, the same intense devotion to place. SkyRim Ranch was a kingdom to her, and she was loyal to it with all her heart.

She was also the only one of the Hale offspring who could be downright rebellious. *That,* her father always said glumly, she got straight from Old Mylo.

Frazier's father, Mylo Swenson Hale, had been independent to a fault and stubborn as a hog on ice. He had lived with them since Abbie was a baby and clearly favored her over her brothers. Abbie, he'd said, had a mind of her own. She reminded him of himself.

Old Mylo had died three months ago after a year of steady failing. His death had deeply shaken Abbie, and his memory haunted her.

He would have laughed at this scrawny colt, she thought with a pang. *He would have teased me unmercifully. But he would have taken my side.*

Now the foal was falling asleep, its head in Abbie's lap, the bottle nearly empty. Gently Abbie removed the bottle and eased away so that the colt's head rested on the bed of straw she'd banked in the porch's corner. She rose stiffly, brushing off her jeans.

Abbie had a pretty face, snub nosed and full lipped, and her dark brows and lashes contrasted with her blond hair. But this afternoon her face was drawn and there were circles beneath her eyes.

She hadn't had a full night's sleep since the colt was born four days ago. Her father kept complaining that anybody other than Abbie would have put the thing out of its misery—or at least let it die as nature had intended.

Frazier complained again now, as he stared down at the colt, whose prominent ribs rose and fell in rhythm with its breathing. "Only you would do this," he said, half in disgust, half in resignation. "Nobody but you."

No, Abbie thought, looking at him stubbornly. *My mother would have done this. Don't you remember? Doesn't the past stay real to you, the way it does to other people?*

A wave of loneliness swept through Abbie; she missed her grandfather, and she still deeply missed her mother, who had been dead for a dozen years. Although she loved her father, lately she resented him. He said she was stubborn and wouldn't see reason. He said she wasn't realistic. He said she wouldn't face facts.

She rubbed her stiff arm and gave him a mutinous glance. He smiled, but she didn't smile back.

"Abbie," he said, as if he knew what she was thinking. "Abbie, things change."

Her blue eyes, usually full of either mischief or determination, went bitter. She knew she shouldn't bring up the subject, but she was too tired to resist. "This is our *home*," she said. "How can you sell it? How?"

He shook his head, as if he, too, were saddened, but there was no help for it. He had put the ranch up for sale and intended to buy a house in town. "A man can fight the inevitable only so long," he said. "I kept it for as long as your grandfather lived. Now it's time to let go."

She stopped rubbing her arm. She dropped her hand and made a fist, but her lower lip trembled. "It's been our home for five generations." Her voice shook with emotion. "And now Grandpa's things... How can you sell Grandpa's things? He *loved* them."

Frazier gave a sigh of strained patience. "Abbie, we've been through this. The boys agree. The ranch's lost money for the past five years. Five years. If we keep on like this, we'll lose everything. Even Old Mylo knew it. I hung on as long as I could, for his sake. But he's gone. So are the old days, when a man could make a living at this. For years there's been talk about Agri-Comm buying out ranches around here and consolidating them. After New Year's they're going to start making offers. That's why I put the place up for sale. I want to get out while we've got a chance."

"The ranch is one thing—and that's bad enough—but Grandpa's collections are another," she retorted. Some stranger poking through them tonight? *Tonight?* You promised nobody would come until after... after the sale. Just keep him away from me, that's all. I don't even want to see him."

"Abbie, I've *tried* to discuss Grandpa's things. You wouldn't listen. Try listening now. I want to avoid estate squabbles. I've seen what they do to a family. It isn't pretty. I can't leave the four of you a couple of *collections*. The boys agree on that, too. We'll sell them, and I'll divide the money equally."

Tears glittered in Abbie's eyes. "I don't want money. It's like you're selling Grandpa's soul. He loved those collections. His stamps, his coins..."

"Stamps don't pay the bills," Frazier said. "And the coins aren't the kind you spend. How much money have you got in the bank?"

Abbie shook her head and kept her mouth clamped shut, not trusting herself to speak. This wasn't a matter of economics or cold logic to her, but one of emotion.

"None," Frazier said, studying her face. "What would happen if I fell over dead? What would you have? Except debts? What could you do?"

She lifted her chin a fraction of an inch higher, but still she did not trust herself to answer. What could she say?

Frazier sighed again. "You'd do just what I'm doing now. You'd have no choice. *I* have no choice. I want you to have some security. And the boys could use money *now*. Why wait until I'm dead? I have to think of them, too."

Abbie looked away, refusing to meet his eyes. She stared at the frost flowers that covered the windows, hiding the December sky. She knew what her father was going to say, and worse, she knew it was true.

Frazier squared his shoulders, and his face was more implacable than before. "John's putting off having a family. Why? Because a professor makes blasted little money. Adon's still paying off his loans for law school. He's got a wife and two kids to support. Preston's got another year of med school *and* his internship. His wife's working two jobs, and it tears him up."

Abbie shoved her hands into the pockets of her jeans. She chewed at the corner of her lower lip. He was right, of course. Each of her brothers could use more money. They deserved better than they had; they were ambitious and disciplined and bright.

They weren't like her. They weren't content to stay at home. They'd always wanted something more than ranch life. She had not, did not. She loved SkyRim.

She stared down at the bony little white colt, sleeping uneasily. It was so frail, so feeble looking that tears started in her eyes. She blinked them back and looked at the frost-covered windows again.

Beyond them, she could visualize the land of their ranch, acre after acre of Nebraska plains, bleak with winter. Perhaps one had to be born on the plains to think such a bare vista beautiful, but Abbie loved the grandeur and sweep of it.

She had never wanted to leave the ranch house and its surrounding land or the wide Platte River that formed the ranch's southern border.

Unlike her brothers, she hadn't been able to stand going to university. After six weeks, hating the crowded campus, hating her cramped room, she'd begged to come home. Frazier had at last taken pity on her.

To please him, she'd enrolled in a few courses at the small community college in nearby Bison City, but her interest in them was forced. Classrooms made her restless.

She liked the outdoors better than any book. She wasn't academically inclined, as her brothers were, and her father always seemed disturbed and disappointed by that fact.

Only her grandfather had approved of her choice. "Why should she listen to some dusty old perfessor? All God's green earth is a lesson. I learnt more geography and politics from collecting stamps and coins than I ever learnt in school. Leave her be."

But now her grandfather was gone, and the life she loved so much was being torn away from her. Her father had made up his mind, and her brothers, who were older and more educated and more successful, sided with him. Her feelings in the matter counted for nothing.

When she spoke again, she struggled to keep her voice under control. "Look," she said. She kept her gaze trained on the frosted glass so she wouldn't have to meet her father's eyes. "I'm tired. Let's drop this. I've got this foal to take care of. And I've got to get ready for Christmas. I can't worry about your precious Connley, too. I'm sorry."

Frazier exhaled sharply. He stared down at the sleeping colt with a disapproving expression that said exactly what he thought of it: *One more problem. One more lost cause.* He looked almost as tired as Abbie felt.

"Go take a nap," he said gruffly. "Get some rest. You've worn yourself out with that damn fool horse."

Abbie shrugged. "Right," she said. Head down, still not looking at her father, she started for her room. He put his hand on her shoulder, halting her.

"Abbie, believe me, I'm doing this as much for you as anybody. I mean that. Truly. At least be civil to the appraiser—to Connley—when he comes. None of this is his fault." Frazier gave her shoulder a slight squeeze. This gesture was the closest he ever came to expressing affection.

Abbie shook her head. She tried a smile but couldn't manage one. It died with a sad twitch at the corner of her lips. "Look, Daddy—" resignation mingled with bitterness in her voice "—you sprang this on me without warning. Selling the ranch is bad enough. But I didn't think I'd have to face the collections being broken up—not for a while. Just...don't ask me to be a good sport about everything, all right?"

A small vengeful demon at the back of her brain was angry that she had to be a good sport at all. It pricked her with its pitchfork and made her add, "Besides, what does it matter what I think? I'll be married before long, anyway. Lucky and I'll have our *own* ranch someday."

She knew Frazier would bridle at the mention of Lucky. Lucky Gibbs was her fiancé, or nearly so. He was a rodeo rider, and Frazier had taken an almost instant dislike to him.

Her brothers, too, derided Lucky, which made her defend him all the more loyally. But Old Mylo had approved of Lucky, and that was good enough for Abbie. "He's got grit, he's got ambition, and he's got brains," Old Mylo had said. "He's got an inquirin' mind. He'll go far."

At the mention of Lucky, Frazier's hand went still on Abbie's shoulder. Slowly he drew it away.

When he spoke, the false heartiness of his tone rankled. "Well, heck, Abbie, if Lucky's going to carry you off and make you happy, why isn't he showing up for Christmas? And where's that engagement ring he's supposed to give you? You think your brothers don't care about you, but at least they're coming home for Christmas. Too bad Lucky can't be troubled."

Abbie knew she had asked for the gibe, but she was tired and her temper flared. She straightened, anger sparking deep in her eyes. She gave her father a withering look. "Don't talk about Lucky like that," she said.

Her father met her gaze without flinching, but his expression was clouded, oddly troubled. "Fine. I'd just as soon never talk about him. Connley's my concern. Don't take out your emotions on him. It's a big job, going through all those coins and stamps. He's coming a long way. So mind your manners—promise?"

She paused. His attitude about Lucky always hurt her, and she was too exhausted to try to be polite. "I won't promise anything. Don't ask."

"Abbie," Frazier began, putting his hand on her shoulder again, "I swear that this is for your own good—"

She broke away from his touch. "I promise nothing," she said from between clenched teeth. "Nothing at all. Keep him out of my way."

IN HER ROOM, Abbie kicked off her boots and threw herself onto her bed. She set her alarm clock to ring in an hour and forty-five minutes, then fell onto her back, one arm across her eyes. Tears of frustration pricked her lids, and she worried that she was too tired to sleep.

Her father said she couldn't ask the foreman, Mingus, to help. Mingus's divorced son, the ranch's other hired man, was in the hospital with a badly broken leg; he wouldn't be home until after Christmas. That left only Frazier and Mingus to haul feed to the range cattle and keep the creeks and ponds broken open for water. The two men were working from dawn to dark.

Abbie knew that her father wasn't cruel, but under pressure he could turn cold and obstinate. The pressures on him were many, and the ranch's economic problems were real. Fewer and fewer families were hanging on to their land.

Nature, Frazier swore, was a harsh mistress. She tried to break rancher's hearts and spirits by springing nasty surprises on them.

The pregnancy of the mare, Sprint, had been one such surprise. For years everyone had thought old Sprint was barren. Then, perversely, at the age of twenty-one, she had gotten herself with foal, and just as perversely, the thing had been born in the dead of winter.

Sprint was a swayback roan with unimpressive bloodlines and no particular talents. Frazier kept her strictly for the sake of Abbie's sentiment: gentle old Sprint had been her mother's pleasure horse.

The ailing foal arrived prematurely and seemed to frighten Sprint. She rejected it. Her very body rejected it; she had no milk for it.

There was another nursing mare, Jetta, who had dropped an autumn foal, a little filly. But Sprint's colt was too feeble to stand and nurse, and he had an infection that threatened to turn to pneumonia.

Frazier had said, cynically, that the colt would die; why try to save it? If by any miracle the thing should live, it would be worthless—its head was plain, its neck was short, it was calf-kneed, its hips and its hocks were too high, and it would be as swaybacked as Sprint.

"Let it die," Frazier had advised. "That's what it's trying to do."

Abbie had thought every single thing he'd said was true—except one. This colt was trying to *live;* she sensed it. In spite of all the odds against it, it wanted to survive. And she was determined to help it.

Abbie had a small hoard of savings from training horses and giving riding lessons. Frazier had only shaken his head when she'd spent it all on veterinary fees and formula and antibiotics.

Now Abbie lay in bed, rubbing her arm across her forehead tiredly. Her head ached for want of sleep. But she had too many thoughts to sort, especially since Frazier had dropped his bombshell. Connley, the appraiser from Lincoln, the state capital, would be flying in *tonight* to evaluate Old Mylo's collections.

Her grandfather had spent over forty years amassing his collections. His stamps and especially his coins were not mere objects to him, they were touched with magic, each with a life of its own. Each had its history, its meaning, its memories, its vital relationship to the others.

Now the appraiser would descend like an evil wizard, turning them back into ordinary lifeless things. Nothing about them would have meaning except their price tags.

Abbie rolled onto her side, clutching her pillow. She put her hand over her closed eyes. Why did the appraiser have to be coming now, when she was exhausted in body and spirit? And why did she and her father have to clash so often these days? And at Christmas, too. The last Christmas the family would have at the ranch.

The frail little colt on the sun porch had become a symbol to her, of all the things she wanted to survive: the ranch and her life there; her mother's memory and her grandfather's, too.

And Lucky, she thought, hugging the pillow more tightly. She knew the struggling little foal, which her father looked upon as merely another of her follies, somehow symbolized her loyalty to Lucky, as well.

Oh, Lucky, she thought unhappily, *why can't you be here for me? I need you. When will you come home to me for good?*

She opened her eyes and stared at Lucky's picture on her night table. It was a photo she'd taken of him at the Ak-Sar-Ben Rodeo in Omaha last year.

In the picture, Lucky was leaning against an empty stock pen. His shirt was the same startling turquoise blue as his eyes, and it stretched across his wide shoulders. His hips were trim in low-slung jeans, and he wore his big gold championship belt buckle—he'd been the Clay Moffett Memorial Bull Riding winner.

His dark hat was tilted at a rakish angle and hid his blond hair except where it grew long in back, curling over his collar. He was giving the camera a sidelong look and a mysterious closemouthed smile. Lucky Gibbs was a strikingly handsome young man, strong, tanned, blond and blue eyed.

"He'd make a helluva pretty girl," her brother Adon had once said sarcastically, but not in Lucky's hearing. Lucky's eyelashes were long, his mouth maddeningly well shaped, and his hair as blond as Abbie's. Though he was not tall, he was as strongly muscled as a little range mustang, and as tough as only a bull rider can be.

Staring at his picture, Abbie managed to smile for the first time that day. Her smile was wan, but real. She'd met Lucky at the Bison City Rodeo a year and a half ago. She'd gone to barrel race, he to ride bulls.

The first time she'd seen him was in the rodeo's grand parade, riding a flashy palomino. The horse had pranced, Lucky had grinned, and she'd been madly infatuated, just like that.

The last night of the rodeo, when Lucky had scored the winning ride, he'd tried to play the comedian and take a mock-heroic bow, thinking the clowns had the bull distracted. But the bull turned on him with unbelievable swiftness. It hooked him at the edge of his rib cage and tossed him against the stadium wall, breaking two ribs and his collarbone.

He'd been off the rodeo circuit for a month, stuck in Bison City. As soon as he was patched up, he spent the rest of that month courting Abbie. Before he'd left, they were unofficially engaged.

"I'll be back for you," he'd vowed. "As soon as I make enough money for us to get started, I'll be back. We're going to have us a little spread right here in Bison County. I promise you that."

A dedicated rodeo cowboy had to be a vagabond and might spend almost 365 days a year taking his chances for the big money. Lucky did the whole, never-ending circuit. He came back to Abbie when he could, but it was never often enough. And he never seemed even close to earning enough money to make the dream of a ranch come true. He hadn't, to Abbie's disappointment, managed to buy her a ring so far. He couldn't even afford to come to Nebraska for Christmas.

Her father said contemptuously that there would never be enough money. Lucky wasn't responsible enough to hang on to it, and he wasn't the sort to settle down.

An odd thought crossed her mind. It came unbidden, and she was ashamed for having it. Her father was selling the collections, dividing the money. She had cried out against such desecration, yet...

How ironic, she thought. What if her father, in his eagerness to settle the estate, gave her enough money so that she and Lucky could buy a small ranch of their own? Lucky could give up rodeoing and marry her—at last.

She sighed, her eyes fluttering shut. No, she thought, she didn't want to think of that. It was disloyal to her grandfather. It was disloyal to her own standards and ideals. But...

Grandpa might have liked that, she thought sleepily. *He'd hate his collection to be split, but he'd like for Lucky and me to be together, no matter what Daddy says. And I'd be on a ranch again and never have to leave it, never....*

But the emotions the thought raised were too complex, too conflicting. She let the idea slip away into nothingness and drifted toward dreamless sleep.

Then, piercing through Abbie's drowsiness, came the memory of the sick little horse, struggling so quietly yet so valiantly for his life. She reminded herself not to sleep too deeply; the foal would need her again, and soon.

"It's going to live," she murmured to herself almost soundlessly. She knew, vaguely, that she meant not just the colt, but any number of things that were precious to her.

"It's going to live," she vowed. "It has to."

But when the alarm woke her an hour and a half later, the colt was worse, far worse.

Its body felt chilled, its half-closed eyelids twitched spasmodically, and its breath rattled and wheezed. The colt was dying.

CHAPTER TWO

No!

Mentally she screamed the word.

In the fading light, the frail white colt already looked ghostly. She pushed the heater closer to him and turned up the thermostat. She ran to her bed, stripped off the blankets and carried them to the porch. She threw them over the little horse's body. It shuddered.

She ran back inside and with trembling fingers punched out the phone number of the veterinarian, Wally Bishop. How she would pay him, she didn't know, but she could not simply watch the colt die.

The next hour and a half passed in a blur. Although in truth Wally Bishop arrived with amazing speed, it seemed to Abbie that he took an eternity to get to SkyRim. He examined the colt and grunted unhappily.

He shot antibiotics into the fragile body with syringes, then he administered another sort of medication through a nasogastric tube inserted in the colt's nostril. Abbie winced in sympathy for the animal and wondered bleakly if her father wasn't right—was she simply increasing and prolonging the animal's misery?

The longer Wally worked with the foal, the grimmer his face grew. At last he shook his head and said that the best thing would be to take the colt to an animal hospital with a neonatal unit—but none was close enough.

Abbie's heart lurched in apprehension. Did that mean the colt would die? There was *nothing* she could do?

"The next best thing," Wally said, his voice pessimistic, "is if I took him back to my clinic. I could put him on an IV. But he'd have to be monitored for at least the next twenty-four hours, Abbie, and probably more. I haven't got that kind of staff, and frankly, it'd cost you a bundle. And I still couldn't guarantee he'd pull through."

Abbie swallowed and stared down at the foal. It was conscious, and Wally was struggling to make it drink its formula. It seemed too weak, too weary. The colt looked as fragile and insubstantial as the frost that rimed the windows.

Don't die, Frosty, she thought, barely realizing she'd just named the animal. *Please don't just fade away like the frost.*

Wally, kneeling by the colt, looked up at her. The vet had a round kind face, but the light falling onto the porch from the living room cast ill-boding shadows on it. The lenses of his glasses gleamed like two tiny full moons, blank and without promise.

"There's a third option," he said without enthusiasm. "I almost hate to suggest it. I could jerry-rig you an intravenous setup here. It'd be crude. You'd have to monitor it full-time. It might not do the trick. If this little guy gets pneumonia—and he's close to it, Abbie—he's a goner. You're dead on your feet already..."

The colt raised his head slightly. His eyes opened, flashing her a brief frightened look that showed the whites, then closed again.

I want to live, she could have sworn the colt was trying to tell her. It seemed to be struggling to say, *Don't count me out yet. I've still got fight. Help me.*

Abbie shook her head helplessly. "Oh, Frosty," she breathed. "Poor Frosty."

She straightened her back and jammed her hands into the front pockets of her jeans. "Do it," Abbie told Wally. "Do whatever you have to. I can't give up on him. I won't."

Wally sighed. "Abbie, you're already worn-out. Your father's going to scalp me for doing this."

"I'll worry about my father," she said brusquely. "Just do it, then tell me what I have to do."

Wally sighed again. But he bundled up, went to his van and came back with his arms full of instruments that looked like torture devices. He set up a stand with a bag of fluid containing antibiotics.to fight the colt's infection. He inserted a catheter in a vein in its neck and taped it in place.

Wally showed her how to replace the bag. He told her he'd trust her to give the colt a shot every four hours. She was a ranch girl, after all. She could give an animal a shot.

In addition, the colt would have to be tube fed its formula every two hours. And if it felt a surge of strength or had a seizure, Abbie had to keep it from thrashing about and pulling out its catheter.

Numbly she nodded. Wally hauled bales of hay from the barn and helped her make a U-shaped wall of hay around the foal that would help keep the chill away and give the animal a sense of shelter, as well.

When Wally was ready to go, he stared down at Abbie, his bland face troubled.

"I still don't know if I should have done this," he said, shaking his head. "And Abbie..."

She looked up at him questioningly.

"Don't get your hopes up," he said gruffly. "You can't win them all. Nobody does."

She lifted her chin, pretending to be far more confident than she was. "I know," she said, trying to sound philosophical.

"I hope so," Wally said bleakly. He adjusted his hat, pulling the earflaps down. He wrapped his muffler around his mouth, picked up his black bag and trudged toward the door.

Abbie went with him, although she first cast a nervous glance over her shoulder at Frosty. He lay still, except for an occasional shiver.

At the front door, Abbie put her hand on Wally's jacketed arm. "About payments—" she began awkwardly.

Wally cut her off. He turned up the collar of his jacket. "We'll work something out," he said. "My kid's been begging for real riding lessons. I guess she's old enough. I might let her have 'em in the spring. We'll talk then."

He squared his shoulders against the cold waiting for him and left Abbie alone in the living room. She heard the door of his van slam, then the engine start and the grumble of tires on gravel as he pulled away.

For the first time, it occurred to her to wonder where her father was. She'd assumed he'd been doing chores, along with Mingus. But it was almost seven o'clock now, past supper time. What was he going to say when he saw that the colt was hooked up to an IV? And where on earth could he be?

Then she remembered the appraiser. Mentally she cursed the man.

She ran her hand through her hair, which was still tangled from napping. Frazier was probably at the airport. He had to pick up his precious city boy, Connley, who probably had dollar signs in his eyes, computer chips in his heart and a price guide in his brain.

She sighed. At least now she had good reason to stay away from Connley. She would be camped out on the porch until Frosty got well—or died.

No, she told herself obstinately, Frosty wasn't going to die; she wouldn't let him. She went into her brother Adon's old room, forcing herself to hurry. She was so tired her gait was unsteady, slightly drunken.

From Adon's closet shelf, she took down his sleeping bag. What little sleep she could steal, she would take on the porch next to Frosty. On her way back to the porch, she snatched up a sofa pillow and took her jacket from the entryway closet. The porch, even with the heater, was chilly.

She checked on Frosty, then slipped back in to her room and got her alarm clock. She could not afford to miss feeding the colt, giving him his shots, or replenishing his IV fluid.

She paused in the kitchen only long enough to seize a can of cola and a box of stale pretzels. She could not remember when she had eaten last. It seemed as if it must have been in another era, possibly on another planet.

SHE DOZED. She awoke at nine and fed Frosty, who, weak as he was, clearly didn't like being tube fed. Then she dozed some more. She awoke and fed him again at eleven, replaced the empty IV bag with a full one and gave him his shot. Her father was still not home. She was too tired to wonder why.

The porch had grown colder, even though the heater was turned as high as it could go. She moved her sleeping bag from the floor at the foot of Frosty's bed and put it down, next to his back. Maybe, she thought groggily, her body heat would help keep him warm.

She dozed until one, awoke and fed the colt again. Then once more she lay down on the straw next to him. She could feel the colt's warmth and hoped he felt hers. She slept.

In her dreams, she was not lying on a cold porch next to a dying colt, but was in Lucky's arms, safe from all loss, all harm. Lucky was strong as love itself. He would protect her from everything.

THE PLANE, delayed by weather for hours, had finally arrived at what Bison City rather grandly called its airport. The plane was a modest prop one that could carry only thirteen passengers; it was the largest sort of plane that landed in Bison City.

One lone passenger had been on it, sitting in seat thirteen. He wore a three-piece suit, an overcoat and expensive gloves, and carried a portable computer the size of a valise. He exited the plane, hunching his shoulders against the bitter blast of the wind, and strode across the tarmac toward the small terminal.

Through the terminal's big windows, edged with frost, he saw a solitary figure waiting with an air of weary impatience. A big older man in a bulky jacket, boots and a dark cowboy hat.

Yates Connley pushed open the door into the terminal's waiting area, and a cold gust of air followed him like a wraith. His gaze met the steel blue ones of the waiting man. The other's face was weather-beaten, the eyes narrowed, even though shaded by the wide brim of his hat.

Yates gave the man a curt unsmiling nod. "Frazier Hale," he said. It was a statement, not a question.

The other man nodded in reply. "Michael Y. Connley?"

"Yates," he said. "The name I go by is Yates." For a brief moment Hale looked him up and down, taking his measure. Yates returned the look in kind, his eyes as dark as the nighttime Nebraska sky. Hale was the first to look away.

"Luggage?" Hale asked.

Yates nodded.

Frazier Hale shrugged and cast a glance down the deserted airport hall toward the baggage-claim area. It was still empty. Together, wordlessly, the two men walked to it.

They didn't talk of Connley's delay. Both men knew the reason. A sleet storm in Lincoln had kept the shuttle flight from taking off for hours. It was now after two o'clock in the morning.

The men stood side by side, waiting for the service door to bang open and Connley's luggage to appear. Frazier Hale looked tired, his eyes shadowed, his spine slumped with fatigue.

Connley, in contrast, managed to look lazy and alert at the same time. He was like a professional soldier, at ease but ready to spring into action as swiftly as needed.

Connley wore a light tailored overcoat, but his shoulders were just as broad as Hale's were in the bulky jacket. Even in dress shoes, he stood an inch taller than Frazier did in cowboy boots. His curly black hair was conservatively short, expertly barbered.

Frazier cast him a sideways look, not altogether friendly. "Figured you'd be older," he said.

"I've got experience," Yates said without emotion. He was thirty.

"And *you're* the right man for the job?" Frazier's voice was dubious. His gaze was trained on Yates's right ear. He must have just noticed the small hearing aid.

"They say I am."

Frazier passed a hand over his eyes. "Sorry. I'm not real courteous, I reckon. I'm tired. Sleeping in one of those blasted plastic seats in there...well, it's hardly possible. I'm a man who likes to stretch out."

Yates nodded noncommittally. He usually needed little sleep and could take it like a cat, anywhere, anytime. He had not, in fact, slept in the past eighteen hours. He'd been finishing up his homework on a hot-check artist.

He was still a detective these days, but at a desk, which he hated, and no longer on the streets where the real action was. He intended to leave that boring desk soon, go into business for himself. But now he had a chance to finish the Claridge case, and it seemed fitting. It was why he had come to these windswept plains.

With a grating clash, the big metal doors opened from the outside. A blast of cold air rolled in, and an airport worker, bundled up as if he were fighting Arctic cold, unceremoniously hurled Yates's two suitcases into the luggage area. The doors clanged shut again.

Yates reached for both bags, but Frazier took one and insisted on carrying it. He gave Yates's tailored coat a doubtful glance. "I hope you don't mind riding in a truck."

"I've ridden in worse."

"You eaten? I been here since seven. Had a couple of those hot dogs they sell. Terrible things. Avoid 'em if you can. I can rustle you up something at home, though."

"I'm fine."

Frazier pushed the door open and led Yates to the parking lot. The icy air closed around Yates like a giant fist, squeezing the air out of his lungs. *Lord,* he thought, watching his breath plume up into the black night. He remembered nights as cold as this, and the memories gave him an unexpected pang.

Frazier threw the luggage into the back of his pickup truck and covered it with a tarp. He offered to take what he probably thought was a valise, as well, but Yates shook his head. "Computer," he said. "I'll carry it."

"That little thing?" Frazier said, frowning. "You one of these computer fellows, too?"

"When I have to be."

Frazier sighed as if to say the world was becoming too complicated for the likes of him. He unlocked the pickup and both men got in. The interior of the truck was as cold as the heart of a glacier.

Frazier put the truck into gear, and it lurched into motion. Soon the airport and its lights disappeared behind them. Yates narrowed his eyes and stared through the windshield. Aside from the gray strip of highway, the world seemed to consist of two dark planes, earth and sky, barely distinguishable from each other.

"How many people at the house?" he asked, studying the featureless sky.

"Just me and my daughter." Frazier shifted his shoulders uncomfortably. "But my sons are due home soon." He was silent a moment.

"My daughter," he said reluctantly, as if broaching an unpleasant subject, "she isn't happy about this."

Yates gave a noncommittal shrug. He knew about the girl. He'd talked to Adon Hale, her brother. Adon worked in the state attorney's office. Nobody there could do anything official yet. There was no hard evidence, and Adon himself wasn't sure how to look for it. But he'd remembered the Claridge case and gotten in touch with Yates.

As soon as Adon had told the story, Yates had got a cold hard knot of certainty in the pit of his stomach. He knew that this was the break he'd been waiting for. He knew he'd be going to SkyRim to check it out, even if he had to go on his own time, at his own expense.

Adon Hale had been frank: his sister would resent a stranger meddling with her grandfather's possessions. She was protective—out of sentiment, Adon said. She was a very sentimental person, Adon said. That's how Lucky Gibbs had gotten to her in the first place.

"I'm sorry to say," Frazier muttered, "that she may be less than polite. She's already on edge about me selling the place. This business about her grandfather's things—it won't go down easy with her."

Yates kept staring into the darkness. "I can handle her." He said it without braggadocio, without any emotion at all.

Frazier cast him a skeptical look, but Yates was unfazed. He was cynical about people. They were all too easy to fool. The girl should be easy.

"She gets set in her ideas," Frazier said.

"I've handled all kinds," Yates said. He had, from murderers to numbers runners.

Frazier raised an eyebrow. "Yeah?" he said dryly. "Well, you've never handled Abbie. She's headstrong. Right now she has a horse on the porch."

Yates shrugged. "Just so she doesn't know the real reason I'm there. I don't want her warning Gibbs."

"She'll blame me for this, too, I suppose," Frazier muttered unhappily.

Yates let the man grumble. He made no comment. He reached inside his suit jacket to make sure he had his glasses. They were there, in their stiff new case. He put them on, supposing he should get used to them.

Frazier droned on, and Yates listened. He listened carefully, because he was interested in the girl and what she might know.

He was sure, from what her brother had said, she wasn't an accomplice. She was innocent, a victim herself. Yates knew that what he was going to prove would hurt her, but he was dispassionate about it. It couldn't be helped.

In the meantime, he had to win her trust and possibly her help, so he had to try to seem friendly and harmless. He'd create the illusion that he was bland, guileless, incapable of threat. And he would not get involved with her. It wasn't professional.

He had come to these bleak plains for one reason: to find the evidence that would bust Lucky Gibbs. He would see that little bloodsucker put behind bars for a long time.

The state of Texas had wanted Gibbs but couldn't make its case. Now the state of Nebraska wanted him, and Yates was the merciless—if unofficial—instrument of its justice. Gibbs, he hoped, was about to be finished.

Lucky Gibbs, he knew with cold certitude, was the man he'd been looking for all these months. There had been only one person connected with the Claridge case they hadn't been able to nail—the man they'd nicknamed the Enforcer.

Gibbs, traveling all over the States and Canada fit the profile perfectly. Nobody had ever thought of a cowboy, for God's sake, not in an operation as sophisticated as Claridge's.

Yes, Yates felt the rightness of it in his bones: Gibbs was the one they wanted, the one who'd been the courier of the stolen goods, the one who'd been the strong-arm man.

Yates wanted him for professional reasons, but he wanted him even more for personal reasons. In the shadows and chaos of the night they'd taken Claridge, someone had fired a gun two inches from Yates's head, then escaped. Yates had been lucky, he supposed, merely to be partially deafened, not killed. But, thanks to the gunman, he'd never be on the streets again.

Now, at last, the gunman had a name. All Yates had to do was tie Gibbs into the Texas business, and he'd as good as have the little SOB. Gibbs was using the girl, Yates was sure. The irony amused him—he would use her, too, to get Gibbs once and for all.

Vengeance, thought Yates bitterly, was going to be sweet. And he'd waited for it a long, long time.

IT SEEMED to Abbie that the alarm went off mere minutes after she had set it. She blinked groggily and stared at its luminous face.

Could it be three in the morning already? Her limbs felt as heavy as stones. Numbly she rose and turned on the porch light. Her fingers, cold, seemed to belong to someone else. Frosty struggled feebly against her ministrations, as if she was hurting him, and tears of frustration bit at her eyes.

By the time she'd finished, her arms shook from the effort she'd spent. Her fingers had become awkward and blundering again.

She managed to set the alarm clock for the five-o'clock feeding, then collapsed back onto the straw, snuggling up against Frosty's body beneath the blankets.

It vaguely occurred to her that her father had been gone and that he should be home now, but she hadn't the strength to go check. All that mattered was sleep. Sleep and the colt.

The pulses in her temples seemed to beat out a mantra of things that counted. The land. And sleep. The colt. And Lucky.

She fell asleep again to that comforting rhythm. The land. And sleep. The colt. And Lucky.

THE MINGLED SCENTS of coffee and bacon woke her. Opening her eyes, she raised her head, confused and disoriented. Beside her, Frosty kicked ineffectually, disarranging the blankets.

Lights shone in the living room and the kitchen. The morning stock report came from the kitchen radio, the announcer droning out the prices of steers, calves, hogs and fat lambs.

Abbie rose on her elbows. The doors from the living room to the porch had been opened, the warmth of the house spilling out over her and Frosty. Abbie was hardly cold at all. And she wasn't hallucinating—aromas of food and coffee truly were wafting from the kitchen.

She turned her back to the door and looked at Frosty. He still lay on his side. He kicked feebly, once more, and this time he tried to toss his head, as well. She put her hand on his ribs, stroking him to quiet him.

The rhythm of his breathing seemed stronger and more even. She sat up, still soothing him. His eyelids fluttered, like a cranky child being awakened too soon.

He's better, she thought with a wave of awed disbelief. *He's really better.* She would have hugged him around his neck if she hadn't been afraid of displacing the catheter.

She stretched and blinked. It was five o'clock, and curiously, this sleep had refreshed her more than her other uneasy naps. She would feed Frosty, then go into the kitchen for a cup of the delicious-smelling coffee. Her father was up early this morning.

How unlike him to brew coffee, she thought. If left to his own devices, he always made instant. And how unlike him to fry bacon. If cooking his own breakfast, he seldom attempted anything more complicated than toast. And why was he having breakfast before chores, instead of after?

Abbie stretched and saw her shadow move, too, cast on the hay bales by the light pouring through the living room doors.

And Daddy opened the doors, she thought, pleased. He'd said it was foolish, pouring heat out into the cold, wasting it on a dying colt, but, bless him, he'd had a change of heart.

She stretched even more luxuriously. Then she was startled to see her shadow swallowed up by a larger one.

Her surprise faded, and she turned, smiling sleepily, expecting to see her father. He was being unusually kind, and she would thank him...

Her lips parted in surprise, then in alarm.

A strange man stood in the doorway, one hip cocked, his feet apart, his arms at his sides, staring down at her.

She sprang to her feet, half crouching, as if ready to flee or attack, whichever proved necessary.

He was a man even taller than her father, and his shoulders were just as broad, but he was far leaner in waist and hip and thigh.

She could not see his features, because the light was behind him. But she could tell his hair was thick and short, and that his clothes seemed to be city clothes, not ranch clothes.

"How are you?" he asked. His voice was deep, slightly gravelly, and made Abbie's spine prickle. She could hear no regional accent in it; all she could think, in her confusion, was that it was a *city* voice.

"How's the colt? Want some coffee?"

Who are you? Abbie wanted to scream. *How did you get in my house? What have you done with my father?* Her mind was so stunned she could not help adding an illogical and unrelated question: *And why are you making bacon?*

He reached over and switched on the porch light. The sudden brightness hurt her eyes, and she gave him a malevolent squint, one she hoped was full of warning.

She didn't know who this man was, but if he had hurt her father, she would rise up and smite him to the ground by the sheer force of angry will. She didn't care how big he was.

She squared her jaw dangerously. "Who—?"

"Connley," he said, cutting her off. "My friends call me Yates." He paused, as if waiting for his name to sink in.

She stared at him without comprehension. Her jaw stayed set at a threatening angle, but wariness crept into her eyes.

"The appraiser," he said. "I came about your grandfather's collections. My plane was delayed. I got in late."

The appraiser. Of course. The tension in her body lessened. She relaxed her sprinter's stance and sank to her knees. She was still full of coiled energy, however, and her expression was distrustful as she scrutinized him.

She had been right about his size. He was a large lean man. She seldom felt comfortable around large men. They reminded her of her father and brothers, almost intimidating. Lucky was only a few inches taller than she. She liked that; it made him seem less alien, more like her.

But similarity between this man and her brothers ended with height. He was dark, rather exotic looking, with swarthy skin and curling black hair.

His eyes and their straight dark brows were black, too. He looked Mediterranean in descent, possibly Italian. Bison City was composed mostly of fair-haired people of German, Scandinavian or Slavic descent. This man's darkness was foreign to Abbie.

His features were even, yet somehow harsh with an innate toughness. Once again, she thought he resembled an

Italian—no, she amended, a Roman, like the ancient statues.

But not any of the pretty, bland-eyed sculptures. Not the statue of a politician or a poet. No, his was the face of...a charioteer, perhaps. A man whose ability to concentrate showed clearly in his steady gaze.

Don't be silly, she told herself. That look of power in him was an illusion, a trick of the light. He might be tall, but she was mistaken about his aura of toughness. For one thing, his glasses worked against it.

He wore steel-rimmed glasses with perfectly round lenses, the kind once called granny glasses and fashionable again among city types. For another thing—she squinted in disbelief—he was carrying a spatula and wearing an *apron*. It was an organdy apron with a ribboned frill at its hem. It looked ludicrous on him.

"Why are you wearing my apron?" she said, sitting back on her heels and putting her hands on her hips. Her brother Adon had given her the apron last Christmas as a joke. Abbie would never have dreamed of wearing such a frivolous thing.

Yates Connley gazed down at the apron as if he'd forgotten he was wearing it. "It was all I could find," he said mildly.

She shook her head and pushed her hair back from her face. He was trim and spotless in clothes far too formal for rural Nebraska. He wore dark gray slacks and a long-sleeved pale blue shirt. A buttoned suit vest matched the slacks. He also wore a tie, but it was loosened, his only concession to informality.

What a dude, Abbie thought, all fear of him vanishing. The more she stared at his glasses and apron and spatula, the more her first impression, that he was rugged, possibly even menacing, faded.

"What are you doing in our kitchen?" she challenged. "Why are you cooking?"

He shrugged. It seemed a mellow-tempered gesture. "Your father said to help myself. Besides, I thought you might be hungry. He said you've been taking care of this...this..."

He pointed the spatula at the sleeping Frosty.

"Colt," Abbie supplied with disgust at his ignorance. "It's a colt."

"Whatever," he said, rather primly.

"Where's my father? It's five o'clock in the morning. Are you going to wake up the whole house because you've got the munchies?"

He put one hand to the frame of his glasses and stood staring down at her, a studious pose. He didn't seem in the least rattled. "It isn't five o'clock," he said. "It's seven. Your father's doing chores. He said to tell you he'd take care of the horses." He pointed the spatula at Frosty again. "Except of course, for that one."

For a moment Abbie stared at him in disbelief. Then she snatched up the alarm clock and stared at it, a wild look in her eyes. It said two minutes to seven. She turned and gaped at the IV bag. It was nearly empty.

"Four hours?" she cried in horror. "I slept *four* hours? Omigosh—I missed Frosty's feeding. He's so weak. If he dies, it's all my fault. I can't believe I—"

"Not to worry," Yates interrupted calmly. "Your father fed the thing."

Abbie drew back and stared at him dubiously. "My *father?*"

"Your father. He's the one who opened the door so the heat from the house could get to you. He's not an ogre, you know. He's concerned about you."

Abbie rose on unsteady legs and began to change the IV bag. She cast Yates another skeptical look. "He wasn't so concerned yesterday. He said he wasn't going to spend good money to warm this porch. It'd only leak outside, and he wasn't about to heat all of central Nebraska."

"That was then. This is now. You weren't sleeping there before—just the horse was."

Abbie changed the bag, deeply grateful to her father. Four hours of sleep seemed like an infinity of rest after the work of the past days.

She fed Frosty again, certain he was feeling better because he was beginning to fight her. Feeding was a hard and a messy job.

Yates, watching her struggle, asked if he could help, but she firmly told him no. He looked plenty strong enough, but he'd make a botch of it. The job took a knowledge of horses. What could Mr. Eyeglasses-and-Apron do, except dirty himself and his expensive clothes?

When she finished, Frosty's little stomach looked almost round. He settled back against the straw and, sated, slipped into an easy sleep.

Abbie stood, gazing down at the colt fondly. Her hair hung in her eyes, and wisps of straw clung to her jeans and jacket.

"Hungry?" Yates asked her, peering at her over the rims of his glasses. "Ready for that coffee? Or do you want to clean up first?"

She looked down at herself. She supposed she was a fright. Well, what did it matter? she asked herself sensibly. There was nobody here to see her except this dandified city slicker.

"I shouldn't leave him," she said, pushing her hand through her hair again. "I should stay close. I'll eat out here."

Yates surprised her by stepping forward and taking her by the arm just above the wrist. "Come on," he said gently, "go take a shower. I'll watch him."

He was as strong as he looked, Abbie thought with surprise, but the expression on his face was stuffy and strait-laced. He made a *tsk-tsk* sound. "Look at him," he said, nodding at the colt. "He's out like a light. He's not about to get into any trouble. And look at *you*. You're hardly fit to handle *his* food, let alone yours."

He grimaced slightly and held her at arm's distance. At his expression of distaste, Abbie smiled sheepishly. His nostrils were pinched and the line of his mouth disapproving.

She hadn't changed clothes since...she couldn't remember. Yesterday morning? Her hair was full of snarls and straw; a shower sounded like heaven.

As priggish as this tall man seemed, staring over his glasses at her, he was right. Frosty was sleeping soundly. Surely she could leave him for the time it took for one brisk shower.

She glanced at the manicured hand on the arm of her crumpled jacket and gave a self-conscious laugh. Yates Connley was such a priss that he probably wouldn't let her into her own kitchen if she didn't wash.

"You win," she said and raised her face to smile at him in gratitude. "I won't take but a minute..."

Her words died away. Her smile, too, died.

The line of his mouth no longer looked prim, but fierce with control. His eyes, in spite of the grannylike glasses, no longer looked disapproving. They looked hungry and full of dark fire.

His hand tightened around her wrist almost possessively. Once again he reminded her of a charioteer or a warrior, not some glorified accountant.

A shuddering wave of awareness passed through her, chilling her and warming her at the same time. Her stomach curled into a fluttering knot.

Then, as if she had seen an illusion, his face grew standoffish again. His mouth thinned into a proper puritanical smile, and his eyes held no emotion whatsoever.

He released her wrist with an over-nice flourish. "Off to the showers with you, miss," he said. "And I'll have a good, hot breakfast waiting. Then I've got to get to work, too."

Abbie searched his face, wondering if her eyes had tricked her. Had that fleeting transformation been the work of her imagination? Had he actually changed, or had fatigue altered her perception of him?

Troubled, she turned away from him and made her way to her room to gather up clean clothes. Her arm tingled oddly where he had touched her. No, she told herself, she only imagined it did. She was tired, that was all. But still her arm tingled as if pricked by hot and cold needles.

She glanced at Lucky's picture on her night table. He still looked at her with his blue-eyed gaze and smiled his enigmatic smile. He seemed ready to tell her some secret—or to hear one from her lips.

She felt odd, off-balance, not quite real. "That man's very...strange," she breathed, barely conscious that she'd uttered the words.

She kept staring at Lucky's handsome face.

Why? he seemed to ask. *Why are you thinking of him, Abbie? You should be thinking of me. Only me. I'm the one you love. Never think of any man but me.*

CHAPTER THREE

YATES SWORE under his breath. He cursed the whole situation, and he cursed his lapse.

He'd been trained never to let down his guard. What in hell had he done? What had happened in that instant he'd held her arm and stared down into her eyes?

He took off the stupid glasses and rubbed his eyes. Too little sleep, he told himself. Maybe sleeplessness was starting to get to him these days. Besides, he wasn't used to this kind of assignment.

Once he'd specialized in going undercover—but always with criminals. This sort of mild, unperiled domestic job was new to him. It should be easy in comparison, but he was finding it distasteful.

His mind flashed back to the moment he'd turned on the porch light. He'd caught Abbie off guard, as he'd intended. But he'd taken one look at her sleepy upturned face, and had been caught off guard himself—badly.

He'd stood there—him, once the best undercover officer on the force—staring at that woman, and all he could think was: *most beautiful.*

A dumb thing to think. But he'd thought it, anyway. She'd worn rumpled jeans and a denim jacket. Her hair was tousled, her face bare of makeup. She was covered with wisps of straw and horsehair.

But she was beautiful. And Adon Hale hadn't warned him. Adon hadn't said one damned thing about his sister being gorgeous enough to stop a man's heart.

Her face was a perfect oval, her lips full and pink and inviting. Her eyes were a sleepy twilight blue. Her nose was delectably snub.

Her corona of hair was thick and rich and gold. She was small, but long legged for her height. She'd tried to hold her back straight, but the slump of her shoulders showed fatigue, and her eyes were shadowed.

She was obviously dead on her feet. Yet she was still the most beautiful thing Yates had ever seen. And when he'd touched her, well . . .

Steady, Connley, he told himself. He'd never gotten involved with a woman on a case, and he didn't intend to. He'd had a perfect record up to now, and he wasn't about to fumble it, not when he was so close to leaving the force.

Once more he put on the wire-rimmed glasses. They pinched the bridge of his nose. Good. He deserved it. He also deserved this asinine apron and the spatula. He swore again and went to stir up a batch of scrambled eggs.

He cracked them one-handedly. He was a decent cook. He was also as hard-nosed a cop as they came, and he sneered at his unexpected reaction to the girl.

So she was a looker? So what? He would keep his emotional distance. Anything else was stupid.

Other men had warned him, especially when he'd been on the streets. You can't always keep your cool, they'd said. You swear you won't get involved, but you do. One day she comes along, and she's different. She gets to you. . . .

Not me, Yates had always thought. He was still immune, he assured himself. He had a job to do. He would do it and be gone.

Getting the proof, that was his assignment. Show that Gibbs had actually stolen coins from Old Mylo and ascertain how much he had stolen. The Claridge ring was broken. Now Lucky had been dumb enough to start working on his own.

Yates needed to prove two things. First, that Old Mylo had once owned coins such as those that had turned up in Texas and were linked to Lucky Gibbs. To do that, Yates needed an inventory, preferably one done before Gibbs had arrived on the scene. Secondly, Yates had to make sure those same coins were no longer in the collection—that they'd disappeared.

Adon had put Yates in touch with his father. Frazier had been cooperative when Yates had phoned, but said he was ignorant of the details of Old Mylo's collections. Stamps and coins had always bored him, he'd said. He'd never paid attention to them.

Adon had been able to tell Yates little more. Adon said the old man had kept strict but screwy records; every item in his collections was supposed to be accounted for and numbered according to his own bizarre system. In the last year of his life, he'd amused himself by transferring those records to his new toy, a computer. But like their father, Abbie's brothers had never taken interest in the collections.

Abbie alone had some familiarity with the coins and stamps—until Lucky came along. In retrospect, said Frazier, Lucky's interest seemed more than casual. Abbie didn't understand much about the computer. Did Lucky Gibbs? Nobody could say. Abbie knew the combination to Old Mylo's safe. Did Gibbs? Frazier didn't think so, but he couldn't *swear* to it.

If the computer records had been meddled with, Yates would have a devil of a time. He'd have to do a painstaking inventory of the collections themselves and pray Abbie had terrific—and honest—powers of recall about what Old Mylo had owned.

Great, Yates thought grimly. All he had to do was get her to cooperate. He just couldn't let her know he was doing it to get that pretty faced little tough, her boyfriend, into jail.

Of course, she'd eventually learn why Yates was there. And then she'd hate his guts. He couldn't blame her. He supposed, from her point of view, he'd come to smash her dreams.

He heard the bathroom door opening; she must be through. He tightened his tie, then straightened it. God, he hated being duded up like this. But everybody had said he looked more like a quarterback than an appraiser, and he needed to diffuse any suspicions Abbie might have. The last thing he wanted was for her to warn Gibbs.

He poured the eggs into the skillet as her footsteps padded down the hall. *Come to Uncle Yates, honeychild,* he thought cynically. *I'm going to play you like nobody's played you—except Lucky Gibbs. And I'm going to play you even better.*

But when she rounded the corner, then stood facing him, all clean and fresh and pretty and sweet smelling, something lurched deep within him, powerfully and painfully. He wished he had a different day's work cut out for him, one that didn't mean every word he was going to say to this woman was a calculated lie.

There was no help for it, he thought, and forced himself to concentrate on deceiving her as completely as possible. It was what he had to do. Justice—and vengeance—were what he wanted, and he intended to have them. A woman's hate was a small price to pay.

ABBIE HAD TAKEN no pains with her appearance. She'd wasted too much time in the shower, luxuriating. She'd shampooed her hair and rinsed it until it squeaked.

She'd blown dry her hair, letting it fall into its natural waves, not bothering to style it. She put on no makeup other than a dash of lipstick. She slipped into clean jeans and an embroidered blue work shirt, put on her fur-lined moccasins and rejoined Yates.

His expression was almost pained when she walked into the kitchen. He stared at her so strangely that she supposed she was slovenly, even hideous, to someone as well-groomed as he was. He turned his attention to the eggs and gruffly told her that she looked nice. But he swallowed hard before he'd said it, so she knew it was only a polite lie.

Somehow he'd found the better china, the pieces they used for company, and set the table. But Abbie insisted on eating on the porch; she had to keep an eye on Frosty. Yates followed her, carrying his own plate and cup and chatting brightly. He still wore the silly apron.

I was loony to think this man could be dangerous, she thought. *I'm so tired I can't keep anything straight.*

But he did seem a paradox to her. She was used to ranchers and cowboys. In her world, a big strong man rode a horse and wrangled cattle. He didn't serve food to her on a china plate, wear a tie and vest to breakfast, and stay inside all day.

But then she noticed the hearing aid. She wondered— had he had hearing problems all his life? Did they give him reason to live a sedentary clerkish existence?

Too bad, she thought, for perhaps without his glasses— and especially without that too-genial air of his—he might be handsome. Not as handsome as Lucky, of course, but acceptable, if one liked the tall, dark, conventionally attractive type.

At any rate, she thought philosophically, he made satisfactory bacon and eggs and perfectly wonderful coffee. There was that to be said in his favor.

She sat in a white wicker chair that she'd placed so she could watch Frosty as she ate. Yates had settled into the matching wicker love seat to her left. He looked as straitlaced as the most proper banker.

But he was talkative and cheerfully curious. She had expected to resent his presence, but resentment, she found, grew increasingly difficult. He was naturally disarming.

He asked questions about Frosty and listened to her answers so intently she felt almost flattered. The hearing aid apparently did its job; he seemed to have no trouble understanding her. She was surprised when she found herself smiling at him.

"Ah, a smile," he said. "I hope that means we can be friends."

The smile he gave her seemed so shy, so self-deprecating, that Abbie didn't want to hurt his feelings. But her own smile died, and she shrugged noncommittally.

His strong-boned face went painfully earnest. "I know that you're not . . . happy about my being here, about my going through your grandfather's things. I probably seem like a vulture to you. I understand your feelings. I've encountered them before in cases like this."

His guess was so accurate she felt ashamed of herself for her earlier hostility.

"I . . . You're just doing your job, I suppose," she said, looking down at her plate. She was no longer hungry.

He cleared his throat as if he, too, was uncomfortable with the subject. He fiddled slightly with the hearing aid. "Well . . . yes. But there are parts of my job I don't like. Estate business is always a little sad."

She nodded but didn't look at him. Instead, she looked at Frosty. The colt slept soundly, his breathing even and deep. Last night his ears had been laid back limply against his head as if he hadn't strength to hold them up. Now they were up, flicking slightly at the sound of their voices.

Yates gave his thigh a falsely hearty slap. "But let's not talk of sad things. Let's talk of something cheerful. You're getting married, I understand? Your father says you're engaged?"

Abbie nipped at her lower lip and gave Yates a sideways glance. He seemed bright and chipper, eager to please her.

Look at him, she thought, half in irritation, half in pity. *A big strong man like that, sitting there in his silk tie and his apron, wanting to talk about engagements. He should be out with the other men, doing men's work.*

She was disconcerted, too, startled that her father had spoken of Lucky. She didn't know what he'd said, but she supposed it was unflattering, and she wanted to set the record straight. "I'm not exactly engaged," she said. "He has to travel so much..."

"Travel?"

"He's a rodeo rider," Abbie said with a smile of pride. "Professional. But when he can settle down, we're going to get a little spread of our own."

"A rodeo rider," Yates said, sounding impressed. He looked at her over the top of his glasses. "My. Will he be here for Christmas?"

Abbie fought against flinching. She wished he hadn't asked that particular question. "No. He's on the West Coast. He can't make it."

Reaching over, she set her plate on the small wicker table next to the love seat. She knew she should try to eat more, but she couldn't. She laced her fingers together and let her hands dangle idly between her knees.

The colt stirred in his sleep, his legs twitching as if he galloped in dreams the way he could not in real life—yet. But Frosty *would* gallop, Abbie vowed with determination. He would survive, thrive and grow ever stronger. She knew that she alone had faith in that, just as she alone had faith in Lucky.

She suppressed a sigh. She kept hoping that Lucky was only teasing her, that he secretly planned to return for Christmas and surprise her.

She imagined him walking into the house unannounced. Then he would reach into his pocket and pull out a little velvet box and hand it to her. She would open the box, and in it would be a diamond ring, twinkling as bright as—

"He calls a lot, I suppose," Yates said. "The two of you keep the phone company in business, I bet."

Abbie's daydream shattered. Her muscles tautened and she locked her fingers more tightly together. "No, actually. It...isn't practical. We're trying to save money." She shrugged. "You know."

"Anything worth having is worth waiting for," Yates said. "Gad, look at me. I still have on this fool apron. Why didn't you tell me? Can I get you more coffee?"

"No, thanks." She gave him a wan smile.

He frowned as he untied the apron and set it aside on the wicker table. How odd and fragile the frilled organdy looked in his hand, she thought.

He had large, browned, well-shaped hands. They looked so strong it was a pity that he did no more with them than tap at the keys of a computer. She was beginning to feel rather sorry for him. But she was curious, too, about what her father had said.

"I'm surprised my father talked about my—about Lucky," she probed. "He's not exactly fond of him."

Yates adjusted his glasses and smiled sagely. "He's like all fathers. Nobody's good enough for his little girl."

She shook her head. "It's more than that. What did he say about him?"

Yates's smile faded. "Why, nothing. But to tell the truth, he really didn't sound too excited. I suppose he worries about the profession—rodeo, I mean."

Abbie ran her hand through her hair. Yates Connley might be odd, but he seemed so open and friendly that he was easy to talk to. He even seemed genuinely sympathetic.

Suddenly she wished she could really confide in him, confide in anyone at all. She had never admitted to anybody her secret fears about Lucky. Her father and brothers didn't like or trust him. They told her that he neglected her shamefully and took her for granted.

She hotly argued that he didn't; his career kept him too busy to dance attendance on her. She said his schedule was so changeable that he often didn't know until the last minute if he could get to Nebraska. She declared their love was so strong they didn't have to put on a big show of perpetual phone calls and letters and silly presents.

She defended him and never uttered a disloyal word against him. Yet in her heart she was sometimes dismayed by Lucky's nonchalance. She wished he would come back to her more often, call more often, write more often.

Oh, when he was there, though, and when he called, nobody could be more charming. When they'd first become involved, he'd often sent her sweet nonsensical presents—never expensive, of course, but they'd delighted her. Of late, even those small gestures were less frequent.

Deep down, she was wounded he wasn't coming to SkyRim for Christmas. Even if she didn't always agree with them, she loved her brothers and was glad they were coming home. But they, like her father, would say pointed things about Lucky's not being there. No one would take her side.

Everything seemed sad and wrong. This was her first holiday season without her grandfather—and her last Christmas at the ranch, her lifelong home. She *needed* Lucky.

If only he would come. She wouldn't mind if he didn't bring a ring. She wouldn't mind if he forgot to bring a present at all, if only he would just come.

Sometimes she feared that he didn't really love her and that perhaps her own feelings were only a stubborn immature reaction against her father and brothers—but that couldn't be right.

"Abbie?" Yates's voice interrupted her unhappy reverie.

She looked at him in surprise. He'd sounded concerned. A frown line had appeared between his dark brows, and his mouth was set at a worried angle.

"You looked sad," he said, setting his own plate aside. He leaned toward her, his elbows on his knees. "I asked you—doesn't your father like your fiancé's being in the rodeo? Did I say the wrong thing? I'm sorry. sometimes I ask too many questions."

"It's all right—" she started to say, but looking chagrined, he cut her off.

"I—I'm curious about how other people live, that's all," he said, straightening his already impeccably straight tie. "My own life is so...restricted. Stamps and coins. Coins and stamps. But sometimes I catch glimpses of other lives. Exciting ones. Different from mine. I didn't mean to pry."

Once again she felt a wave of something akin to pity for him. Drat, she thought, he really did seem like a nice man, a mild, gentle, harmless soul.

She looked at those ridiculous glasses ruining his handsome face, at the restricting, too-correct clothing that made his big frame seem straitjacketed by formality. How could she have imagined anything dangerous about him? Fatigue, she thought. Fatigue and worry—about the colt, the ranch, the future, Lucky, everything.

"You weren't prying," she said, trying to set him at ease. "You're right. Daddy thinks the rodeo life is for bums or something. But he's wrong. Lucky's a very...a very sensitive person. Daddy just doesn't understand."

"What doesn't he understand?"

How nice, Abbie thought, studying those intent dark eyes behind their glasses. Unlike the men in her family, Yates Connley was someone who asked her questions, instead of telling her all the answers.

"Well," she said, "Lucky's had a hard time."

Yates leaned forward more intently, as if truly interested. His eyes held hers. They were really most extraordinary eyes, Abbie thought in confusion. Deep set, intent, black as onyx, they could be hypnotic if only he was more sure of himself.

She tried to ignore the exotic blackness of his gaze and answer his question. "Lucky hasn't had an easy life at all," she said, feeling oddly breathless. "His family wasn't— happy. His father went to prison when Lucky was twelve. And his mother...well, he tries to laugh about her, but she just wasn't able to cope, really. His big sister kind of went wrong. Nobody in the family's ever amounted to anything, except Lucky and his older brother. His brother works in Omaha, but he's very narrow-minded. He doesn't approve of Lucky—because of the rodeo."

"It sounds tough." Yates put an elbow on his knee and his chin on his fist. He regarded Abbie with what seemed true interest, but she had the strange sensation that he was sometimes letting his glance drift to her mouth.

"It was hard," she said. "Lucky got in trouble when he was young. Nothing serious, but he got sent to a ranch school—a kind of rehabilitation program—and found himself riding, doing ranch work. Then he got into rodeo. He's good. He's really very good."

"A self-made man?"

"Completely. Daddy doesn't appreciate how much Lucky's had to overcome. I mean, he can't understand."

"Nobody handed Lucky anything," Yates said, nodding studiously. He sat up straight again and crossed both his arms and his legs tightly.

"Exactly," Abbie agreed, relieved that he understood. "He's had to do it all himself. He...he has feelings, but he hides them. People who don't know him think he's cocky, but deep down, he's actually kind of insecure."

"Insecure?" Yates said. "I imagine he is, with a past like that."

She nodded emphatically. "Yes. And he's proud, too. That's why he doesn't want...why we won't get married until he's made enough money so we can start out free and clear."

"Sounds admirable to *me*." Yates said, reaching for her empty coffee cup. "Let me get you more coffee. Then I've got to get to work. I brought my own computer, but I'll need to work with your grandfather's system, too. Can you tell me anything about it? Your father doesn't—"

The ring of the phone interrupted him. Abbie sprang to her feet, her face brightening. "Maybe it's him," she breathed as if to herself. She ran into the living room and snatched up the phone, hoping to hear Lucky's voice.

But it was not Lucky on the line. It was Myra Hurley, the wife of a neighboring rancher. She had called to say that Frazier's best young bull had escaped and gotten in with the Hurley stock. Frazier and the Hurley's foreman were trying to straighten out the mess, which was why Frazier was late.

Abbie shouldn't worry; Myra would see that Frazier got a good breakfast. Numbly Abbie thanked her and hung up the phone. She returned to the porch, suddenly aware again of how deeply tired she was.

"Something wrong?" Yates stood by the door, concern on his face.

She shook her head and explained Frazier's delay. Once more Yates offered to refill her coffee, but she shook her head and covered a yawn. "I've got to get a little more sleep," she said. "I've just got to. I'll do the dishes and then—"

"You'll do no such thing," he said firmly. "I'll stick them in the dishwasher. You're worn-out. And don't sleep on that straw again. Curl up on the love seat."

She started to protest, but had to stifle another yawn. Yates stared at her sternly. "To slumberland, miss. I insist. For that little fellow's sake." He nodded toward Frosty.

He was right. She glanced at the love seat, nodded, then knelt, resetting the alarm clock. She picked up her pillow, rose stiffly, then settled down on the love seat, drawing her feet up. With the doors from the living room open and the heater on, it was hardly cold at all on the porch. Despite her disappointment over Lucky's not calling, she began to drift off to sleep almost immediately.

She was hardly aware when Yates returned to her side, or when he covered her with a quilt from Adon's bed and tucked it snugly about her.

She did not know that he stood above her, looking at her for a long time.

ABBIE'S DAY TURNED into a surreal patchwork of hard labor and exhausted sleep. Each time she fed the colt, he struggled with greater strength. By three o'clock, his tenth feeding since the vet had left, Frosty was tossing his head and trying to gather his legs under himself, as if he wanted to stand.

To keep him calm so that he would not dislodge the catheter in his neck, Abbie slept beside him again, one arm draped protectively over his ribs. All her muscles ached, and the cleansing shower of that morning seemed a century ago.

She was vaguely aware that her father was in and out of the house. Once, in the afternoon, she heard him trying to stamp the cold from his feet. Once she thought they'd talked while she fed the colt. He told her she was working too hard—or had that conversation been yesterday? She couldn't remember.

She thought he said he would help her if he could, but the aerator on the big pond in the north range was broken, and he and Mingus had to keep chopping the ice so the cattle could drink.

She was, oddly, more aware of the stranger's presence than her father's. Whenever she saw Yates she was startled by his height, the breadth of his shoulders. But then, when she saw his glasses, his tie and vest, heard his mild inquiries, she relaxed.

It was only that harmless strange duck of an appraiser, she would think. He managed to appear almost every time she rose to care for Frosty, asking if he could help.

Rather grumpily she always refused his offer—what in heaven's name did he think he could do? But his mood stayed genial, and he brought her hot chocolate, and once a bowl of soup and a sandwich, although she was too tired to eat.

She remembered snatches of conversation with him. She always asked, hopeful, if Lucky had phoned while she was asleep. He always shook his head and looked sympathetic.

He asked her when she'd last talked to Lucky. Queerly, she couldn't remember. Had it been a week? More? Lucky didn't even know about the colt yet, of that she was sure.

Seeming kindly, seeming interested, the appraiser asked where Lucky was exactly. Abbie was too tired to lie. She admitted, sadly, that she didn't exactly know. The West Coast covered a lot of territory, and Lucky could be maddenly vague about his plans.

Then Yates had again tried to ask her about her grandfather's computer. Apparently he was having trouble finding what he wanted in its files. Abbie couldn't think straight, let alone contemplate the intricacies of the computer.

Wally, the vet, came again at seven in the evening. Mercifully he took over the feeding duties from Abbie, and she sat groggily on the love seat watching. Wally coaxed the colt to its feet and helped it to stand for the first time. Its gangly legs shook, but with assistance it managed.

"I think you've done it, Abbie," Wally said, giving her a worried smile. He took the catheter from Frosty's neck and cut away the tape. "I'm taking him off the IV. I think he's going to make it. He's still going to need a bottle every two hours. If he stands by himself, you can try him with the mare. He'll need shots every four hours for the next two days. But get somebody to spell you. Or the next doctor who comes out here will be coming for you."

"I can handle it," Abbie protested, but her tongue felt thick, and her words sounded slurred. She had been working with the colt five full days now, and knew neither her father nor Mingus could spare the time to help.

"I can spell her," a quiet voice came from behind them. Abbie, startled, whirled in her seat to look up at Yates. As always, his first appearance disconcerted her. His workday hardly seemed to have so much as creased his shirt. His only concession to comfort was that he had rolled his sleeves to his elbows and slightly loosened his tie. He stood with his hands in the pockets of his slacks, his face solemn and his glasses gleaming in the lamplight.

Wally looked at him questioningly.

"I'm Connley, the appraiser," Yates said. "For the coin collection. I'm here for the next few days. Tell me what to do. I'll do it."

"No," Abbie said and tried to get up.

Yates's hand on her shoulder was amazingly hard and strong. "I said I'll do it," he muttered, keeping her from rising. "I've got to stop staring at that computer some time. And you've got to rest."

Wally, kneeling beside the colt, squinted up at him. "You ever give a shot?"

"Yeah," Yates said. "My grandparents ranched. I can give a shot."

Abbie looked up at him in dull surprise. He wasn't quite in focus, but he seemed subtly different to her. He *sounded* different—harder, more serious, more in charge. She rubbed her eyes, trying to see him clearly. Once again she had the irrational sensation that some kind of danger emanated from this man.

But the thought drifted away, for her head had begun to pound, and no thought seemed strong enough to stay with her for long. Numbly she watched and listened as Wally explained.

At last Wally rose and made ready to go. Abbie, too, started to get up, but was surprised to find that Yates's hand still gripped her shoulder and held her in place.

Wally shook his head as he coiled his muffler around his neck. "Don't bother, Abbie. I'll let myself out. Is your father still doing chores?"

She nodded. It had been a hard winter so far, and hard winters meant endless work keeping the stock safe.

Wally's expression grew gloomy. "You'll both kill yourselves," he muttered. "Don't let him work himself too hard. He's not a young man any longer. And take care of yourself, too."

He left, and Abbie sat, dazed and aching, in the love seat. She was still singularly conscious that Yates's hand clamped her shoulder; for some reason it burned her flesh like a brand. Her temples throbbed harder. Why did his touch make her tingle so wildly? Even Lucky's didn't do that. She frowned, trying to understand.

"Come on," Yates said gruffly. He was in front of her, drawing her to her feet. "It's into the shower, kid. Then I'm going to feed you and put you to bed—a real bed."

"No!" she insisted, trying to pull away. But he was as strong as he appeared, and she was too weary to fight. He turned her around and wrapped one arm about her shoulders. Vaguely she resented the action. Just as vaguely, she found it comforting, for his length felt surprisingly powerful and protective against hers.

He half carried, half propelled her to the bathroom. "The shower," he repeated firmly, opening the door. "Then you eat. Then you sleep."

"No," she objected again, but he pushed her inside, gently yet resolutely, shutting the door behind her.

"He's crazy," Abbie muttered, pressing her fingertips to her temples. But she was disheveled again, and she realized she'd hardly eaten in the last twelve hours. Gratefully she stripped off her clothes and stepped into the shower shuddering with pleasure under the warm cascade of water.

Cursorily she washed her hair again. Stepping from the shower, she felt oddly light-headed. It did not even occur to her to dry her hair. She took her old blue bathrobe from the hook beside the door and bundled herself into it. She shook her wet hair out so that it streamed, water-darkened gold, to her shoulders.

Perhaps she would let Yates take over one of Frosty's feedings. But not the next one. Not any of them tonight. Those feedings would be crucial, and Wally said she must watch the colt closely; she was to phone him if there was any hint of a relapse.

How strange, she thought, opening the bathroom door. For a moment she'd allowed herself be ordered about by that mild-mannered bespectacled desk jockey. She had actually *obeyed* him.

She was surprised to see him standing at the end of the hall, a pot holder in his hand. He looked her up and down. "Don't you have slippers? Your hair's wet. Are you warm enough in that?" He took off his glasses and narrowed his eyes at her. "Are you all right?" he asked, his voice dubious.

I'm fine, she wanted to say, *I'm going to eat, take a nap, then take care of my horse.*

But all she could do was stare at him. Without the glasses, he was very handsome. Exactly like the Roman charioteer she'd thought before. A charioteer with a hearing aid and a pot holder.

"Abbie?" One dark brow rose questioningly. His shoulders tensed.

I'm fine, she tried to say, but suddenly there were two of him standing in the hall, and she couldn't decide which one to speak to; both were darting in and out of focus.

"Abbie..."

She moved her lips to say it: *I'm fine.* No words came. Because both images of him danced crazily in her vision, she tried to move nearer, to see him more clearly. But she seemed to be stepping over a threshold into darkness, nothingness, the floor itself falling away beneath her feet.

Yates swore and stepped forward, catching her unceremoniously in his arms. Abbie sank into them, too dazed to protest. The belt of her robe came undone, and the lapels slipped apart, leaving one shoulder bare.

With a sigh, she collapsed against him, feeling the wool of his vest, the starch of his shirt, the silk of his tie, against her bare skin.

Almost furiously, he swept her up into his arms. Momentarily her vision cleared.

She had the fleeting impression of a coppery-skinned face hovering above hers, with eyes as black as jet and so intent they seemed to suck her soul away.

She yielded to him. She sighed again and quietly passed into unconsciousness.

CHAPTER FOUR

YATES STARED DOWN at the woman in his arms, his heart slamming against his ribs. He framed her chin with his thumb and forefinger, turning her face to his.

The sweep of her lashes was dark against her cheeks, and her pink lips were slightly parted.

She smelled of soap and shampoo and the flowery scent of bath powder. Her hair dampened the front of his vest, seeping through his shirt and wetting his chest.

Her robe had fallen open above the waist. Her right shoulder, bare, rested against his silk tie. She was so light that she felt like nothing in his arms, but the weight of her shoulder scalded his sternum as if someone had pressed a hot stone there, trying to burn it into his heart.

His eyes fell to the pale gleam of her body between the gaping halves of the robe's top. One naked breast pressed, hidden, against his vest. The other was half concealed by the folds of blue cloth. It looked as smooth, white and soft as the petal of a gardenia. Desire heated his body, but he fought it.

Don't look at her like that, his common sense warned. He reached to close the robe.

The weight against his heart increased and burned more hotly as he pulled the lapels closed. The back of his knuckles accidentally brushed one covered breast, barely touching it, yet the touch made him clench his teeth.

With an abrupt motion, he pulled her robe together still more, then shifted her so she lay securely against his chest. Effortlessly he carried her to her bed.

He flicked on the lights and in an instant took in the details of the room. It was exactly what he would have imagined. Pictures of horses or of people with horses hung on three walls, and a fourth was given over to awards: ribbons from fairs and riding contests, mostly.

Holding Abbie close with one arm, he used his free hand to jerk back the spread and blanket from the bed. He lay her down as gently as he could. He was careful not to let her nakedness slip into view again. Its effect was too powerful.

He pulled the blanket up to cover her, then straightened. He realized he had been holding his breath. Uneasily he released it from between teeth that were still clenched.

Her damp hair fanned out against the snowy white of the pillowcase. She made a small moan deep in her throat. Her brow wrinkled slightly, as if she was in pain. Her left hand, lying palm upward beside the pillow, moved slightly, the fingers opening and closing.

She made the same unhappy sound again and stretched her hand across the sheet, as if reaching for something. Instinctively he understood what she wanted—human contact. Against his better judgment, he took her hand in his, lacing his fingers with hers.

His hand was large, hard and dark in comparison with hers. Her fingers tightened around his, then relaxed. Her brow smoothed itself again.

Yates sighed roughly. He drew up a wooden chair and set it backward next to her bed. He straddled it and sat, resting one arm along the chair's back. His other hand he kept locked with hers.

She wanted to hold someone's hand? Okay. She would. He knew that his was not the touch she craved, but in her dreams she might imagine it was. Lucky Gibbs was the man she had been reaching for. The thought knotted his stomach.

The poor kid was crazy for Gibbs. Yates had seen her face light up when she thought Gibbs was phoning. He'd watched the light die when the caller's voice was not his. Every time she'd awakened, she'd asked if Gibbs had called.

She had no hint that the little bastard had probably robbed her grandfather blind. She'd never imagined that her "proud" and "sensitive" boyfriend was a two-faced punk. The reality would hit hard.

He let his dark gaze flick to the picture on her bedside table. Lucky Gibbs's too-pretty face smirked at him across Abbie's sleeping body. Yates squeezed her hand more tightly.

I'm sorry, kid, he thought. But with a pang, he remembered the beauty of her bared shoulder and breasts, the feel and warmth of her when he'd held her in his arms.

She's no kid, and I can't afford to feel sorry. She's no concern of mine.

He let go of her hand. He rose and left the room, flipping the switch, casting the room into darkness.

He moved down the hall, forcing Abbie from his mind. It was late, but he'd go back and battle that computer until it was time to feed the colt. He had a job to do. Back in Lincoln, it had sounded like such a nice clean job. But it no longer seemed either nice or clean. It seemed surprisingly dirty.

Then he touched his hearing aid and remembered why he wanted Gibbs so badly. You could only catch dirty guys by playing dirty yourself.

ABBIE AWOKE to sunlight streaming through her curtained windows. Luxuriously, she snuggled more deeply into the bed's warmth, hiding her face against the pillow.

She half dozed, but the memory of the sun's brightness teased her, trying to draw her from the comfort of sleep. The room had been strangely awash with light for an early winter's morning.

Winter morning? she thought, her eyes flying open. *How could it be so bright on an early winter morning?*

A riot of thoughts tumbled through her mind—Frosty. She should be up feeding Frosty. What time was it? When had she fed him last? She could not remember. Wally had been there, saying the colt was better. Then Yates Connley told her to take a shower, and then things went dark and blank.

Panic surged through her, and she lunged from bed. Her muscles protested, but she ignored their ache. Desperately, she looked about for her alarm clock. It was gone—it must still be on the porch.

She glanced at herself in the dresser mirror. Her cheeks were rosy with sleep, but the rest of her face was unnaturally pale. Her hair was tousled and flyaway, giving off bright sparks of reflected light. She wore only her old bathrobe, its belt undone, and under the robe she was naked.

In dismay she pulled the robe tightly shut and belted it. Why had she gotten into bed like this? Where was Frosty? *How* was Frosty? Had Frosty died while she slept and nobody had wakened her to tell her?

She didn't stop to think. Pushing a hand through her hair, she rushed out of her room and toward the porch. Her father was nowhere to be seen, and the ranch house, except for the haunting aroma of coffee, had an air of emptiness.

With a start she realized that although the house was quiet, it was not truly empty. On the porch, kneeling in the straw, was Yates, holding the wobbling colt upright while it eagerly nursed from its bottle of formula.

She was relieved to see that Frosty seemed fine, far stronger than last night, and greedy for food. He rolled his eyes when he saw her and twitched his tail, but he did not miss a beat in the hungry rhythm of his suckling.

She stopped in the doorway, looking at Yates with something akin to wonder. His glasses had slipped down, and he looked back at her over their tops, his expression guarded.

The sunshine had melted the frost on the windows, and the light came pouring through them, glinting on Yates's curly blue black hair. He wore black dress pants, a blue-and-white pin-striped shirt and a dark blue tie that Frosty had somehow knocked askew. Although his shirtsleeves were rolled up, he'd made no other compromise in his dress. He might have been a Wall Street banker kneeling in the straw, supporting a gangly colt with one hand, grasping the bottle of formula with the other.

The most surprising thing was he held and fed the colt with such an air of sureness. He might be dressed as if he'd just stepped from the pages of *Gentleman's Quarterly*, but he also looked like a man who knew exactly what he was doing.

Abbie shook her head in disbelief. "What *is* this?" she demanded.

He lifted one shoulder and looked away from her. His attention seemed concentrated on Frosty. "Feeding. Have a good sleep?"

Her brow furrowed in perplexity. She could see the alarm clock, but its face was turned away from her. "What time is it?"

He couldn't glance at his watch; his left hand was propping up the colt. He shrugged again. "About eleven-fifteen, I think."

"Eleven-fifteen?" Abbie was confounded. "How long did I sleep?"

He squinted up at the ceiling, as if doing the math in his head. "About fourteen hours," he said, then concentrated on Frosty again. "Attaboy," he said as the colt gulped its meal.

"Fourteen hours?"

He nodded, still not looking at her. "More or less."

"But—but who took care of Frosty? Surely not you... When did you sleep?"

"Your father spelled me for the five-o'clock feeding. I caught my shut-eye then."

Impulsively, Abbie knelt beside him. She studied his profile, looking for signs of fatigue. She found none. He had nicked his chin slightly while shaving, the only hint that his life might not be running in its usual smooth groove.

Embarrassed that he had done so much for her, she didn't know what to make of him. And now he seemed to have gone shy on her; he would not give her so much as a glance.

"How much sleep did you get?" she asked. "Three and a half hours?"

"About."

"You've fed him—what?—eight times?"

"Seven. That's all. Seven."

"You gave him his shots—" she struggled to calculate the number "—four times?"

His only answer was a nod.

"While I slept like a log?"

"You needed it." His voice was without emotion.

She put her hands on her hips, staring at his profile in frustration. "You shouldn't have done that."

"It's done."

"It's not your job—"

"It's *done*."

She sighed. She sank back on her heels. She reached out and stroked Frosty. Her soft sleeve brushed against Yates's starched one. He flinched slightly—or did she only imagine it?

She found herself edging away from him just a bit. It shouldn't bother her to touch him accidentally. She would never be attracted to a man like him, she told herself. Yet some deeper instinct told her to move away, and she obeyed. She found, to her bewilderment, that his nearness made her strangely prickly.

Tentatively she reached out to pet Frosty again, careful this time not to let so much as her sleeve touch Yates. "I don't even remember going to bed," she mused, troubled by the fact. "I remember Wally being here. I remember taking a shower. I remember coming out and standing in the hall. You were there. You had a pot holder...."

Her voice trailed off. Frosty had finished his bottle. Yates drew it away. He let the colt sink back to the straw. It sighed in contentment, its eyes half-closed.

Yates rose abruptly. Abbie did the same, wanting to know what had happened. Why was he acting so strangely? Yesterday he had been the soul of friendliness. Today he seemed uncomfortable merely talking to her.

"You passed out," he said laconically. He straightened his tie and started toward the kitchen.

Abbie stared after him in amazement. Then she followed him. "I passed out? *Me?* I've never passed out in my life. Well, once. I took a fall off a horse and got the wind knocked out of me. But I've never just...passed out."

"You passed out." He washed his hands at the kitchen sink, scrubbing them clean.

"Where?" she asked, bewildered.

He handed her the soap. "In the hall."

She obeyed his unspoken command and washed her hands, soaping away the traces of Frosty. She still couldn't believe Yates's assertion. "How'd I get to bed?"

"I put you there."

She wheeled to face him. He handed her a towel. He put one hand on his hip and stared out the kitchen window.

"You?" she said in disbelief.

"Me."

He turned and looked at her at last. His ebony gaze jolted through her. The set of his face was one of grim control. "Look, I helped you. It's no big deal. Don't thank me, because I have to ask for your help."

"My help?" Abbie still could not cope with the news that Yates had put her to bed. She stared at him, disconcerted, wondering why his black eyes sent such indefinable sensations rippling through her.

"Your help." His gaze held hers. "Your grandfather's computer files are a mess. They make no sense. Your father says you know the collections: At least better than anybody else in the family."

She nodded numbly, not understanding what he meant. A muscle twitched just below his cheekbone.

"To make sense of it, I need your help," he said. "Are you willing to give it?"

Abbie felt oddly breathless, her chest constricted. "Of course," she murmured.

"In return," he said, leaning nearer, "I help you with the horse."

She ducked her head and pretended to take an interest in folding the towel. "I can't let you do that," she began.

"You help me, I help you."

"But you can't do two jobs," she objected. "You'll get all worn-out."

He gave a short ironic laugh. "Yeah? Well, you're already worn-out. I can't afford to lose you. I need you."

I need you. The words made Abbie's heart lurch in a way that was half frightening, half pleasant. "But—"

"We'll eat and talk about it," he said. "You'll fall over again if you don't eat. What kind of sandwich do you want? Roast beef or cheese?"

"Lunch?" she protested. "No. I'll make it. You can't do everything around here. It's time *I* did something." She looked up at him again, full of confusion.

"You can do something," he said brusquely. He jerked his gaze away from her and let it rest on the window again. "Go put some clothes on," he said. The muscle under his cheekbone twitched again.

Abbie's face went hot. For the first time she remembered that under the robe she was naked. She had the sudden upsetting conviction that he *knew* she was.

He said she'd fainted. He said he'd put her to bed. The old robe was baggy, its belt was frayed, it often came undone....

No wonder he's acting so oddly, she thought. *He's embarrassed.* Then she fled from the kitchen, mortified.

ALL RIGHT, all right, Yates told himself. So she'd knocked him off-balance again. So the tricky chemistry between them had changed, become more volatile.

It was nothing he couldn't handle. He'd be more careful. He'd get back into character: sexless, harmless, nonthreatening. A brotherly clerk. A friendly twit.

But damn, he thought, it was hard to feel sexless and brotherly when she'd appeared on the porch with that undisciplined wealth of gold hair shining in the sun as if she were the goddess of morning.

Her blue robe was short—not seductively short—but brief enough to give him an unsettling glimpse of silky-looking legs. Her face had been sleepy, yet beautiful.

All that he must resist. It was merely physical. It meant nothing.

He had to steel himself, and he could do so by thinking of her with Lucky Gibbs. The thought was as harsh as a slap in the face. She was Lucky Gibbs's property. He was starting to loathe that fact.

IT WAS AFTER LUNCH. Yates had seemed more himself again, Abbie thought. Furtively, she cast him a sidelong glance. Now she was seeing yet another side of him: the man at his own work.

They both sat at the long oak library table in her grandfather's study. Yates stared at the computer, his jaw set. His frustration was such that he had actually loosened his tie.

"I can't get it," he said, glaring at the screen. "I just can't get it."

Abbie put her elbows on the table and her chin in her hands. She, too, stared at the uncooperative screen.

"Explain it to me—in simple terms," she said, determined to try to understand the problem.

Yates drew a deep breath. He adjusted his glasses and frowned more intently at the screen. "If he had files on the hard drive about his collection, they're gone. There's a lot of other garbage in there—letters, games, even a story. But no inventory of coins or stamps. None."

Abbie lowered an eyebrow and frowned, too. "Well, he put records in. I remember, because it took him so long. But that was why he kept sending the computer in for repairs. Whole files would disappear from—what is it?—its memory.''

Yates pushed back from the table and crossed his arms. ''Okay. Your father said the same thing. Tell me how you remember it.''

His face was stony, but he seemed to force the harsh line of his mouth to soften. ''Sorry,'' he said mildly. ''I get caught up and I get intense. Just tell me, please. You might remember something he can't.''

He gave her half a smile. Abbie tried to smile back. He didn't have to apologize for being intense, she thought. She rather liked him when he was intense. The thought startled her, and she tried to drive it from her mind.

''My grandfather loved this computer,'' she said. ''He couldn't get around much the last few years. It was like a whole new world to him. It was his last big expenditure.''

Yates rocked slightly on the chair's back legs, his jaw set again. ''Your grandfather had money once.''

''Once. After World War II, he bought land in Oklahoma—sight unseen. Pure speculation. But he was lucky. There was oil on it. He was a cattleman, not a wildcatter, though. He was content to stay right here and let them send him the checks.''

''Right.'' Yates rose. He began to pace the room. ''That's when he started collecting. When the oil money was rolling in.''

Abbie turned her eyes away from him and traced the pattern of the familiar grain of the oak tabletop. ''Yes. The coins first, then the stamps.''

Yates stopped before a bookshelf and picked up the well-worn copy of a book. It was an encyclopedia of valuable coins. He opened it at random. ''After twenty-some years, the money ran out,'' he said. ''So he stopped collecting.''

Abbie kept tracing the grain. "He stopped buying—for all intents and purposes. The oil wells went dry. He'd trade with other collectors—by mail. But he couldn't afford to indulge himself much."

"But once in a while he did?"

"Once in a while."

"So, the collections kept changing because he kept trading? And once in a while, buying?"

"Right. Changing slightly, but changing."

"He was never tempted to sell the collections? Even when the ranch was losing money?"

Abbie shook her head. "No. The collections were like money in the bank to him. He thought the longer he held on to them, the more valuable they'd be. He thought he was leaving us a fortune by keeping them intact."

She smiled with sad irony. She would rather have her grandfather back than have all the money the collections might be worth. She hadn't so much as looked at the coin albums or holders since he'd died. The stamp collection, either. She couldn't. Her sense of loss had already been too deep, too painful.

Yates didn't look up from the book. "The computer was his last indulgence?"

Her smile grew sadder. "Yes. Daddy thought he was crazy. But Grandpa loved it. That's how he had most of his fun—cataloging the collections, making inventory lists. The computer was a new way to do all that."

"Except it gave him trouble?"

"He said it was like falling in love with a bad woman. She kept betraying him. Like I said, whole files would disappear. He'd fuss and cuss and send it to be fixed. The computer people'd send it back and say it was fine. They said he had to be doing something wrong."

"And?"

"I suppose he was. He got forgetful near the end. And full of funny ideas. He didn't even like handling them anymore—the coins or the stamps. I think he got the idea he'd wear them out or something. It was sad to see."

Yates turned to look at her. The afternoon sunlight caught the lenses of his glasses, hiding his eyes. "So he became . . . a little eccentric?"

She gave a rueful laugh. "He'd always been a little eccentric. He became a *lot* eccentric."

He put the book back on the shelf and walked toward her. He stood, looking down at her, his hands in the pockets of his slacks. "So eccentric that he didn't back up his files on floppy discs? Make an extra copy?"

"He made copies of everything." She nodded at two small oak file boxes on the table. They held her grandfather's backup discs.

Yates made a low harsh sound of exasperation. "I've been through them all. There's nothing about the collections on them. Not a thing. They're gibberish."

Abbie looked at him in startled surprise. "What do you mean, 'gibberish'?"

He ran a hand through his dark hair. "He had sixty-two discs with the same thing on them—some weird story about Bucky the Horse."

Abbie's stomach took a sickening dip. "Bucky the Horse?"

Yates nodded grimly. "Your father says Bucky was a horse your grandfather had when he was a kid. That his sister wrote the story. She was about ten at the time."

Abbie swallowed hard and nodded. "His sister Abbie. I was named for her. She died when she was only eleven. A few years later there was a house fire. It destroyed almost all the family souvenirs, pictures, letters, but that story survived somehow. He treasured it."

Yates sat down and looked into her eyes. "Did he treasure it so much that he'd make sixty-two copies of it? That he'd erase all his inventories to recopy it? Had he become *that* eccentric?"

Abbie's eyes stung with unshed tears. "I don't know," she said helplessly. "I don't think so, but in a way I know he never got over losing her. Maybe at the end, he started missing her so much that he kept recopying the story. He was starting to live in the past more and more. But I didn't think it was that bad."

Yates studied her reaction. He looked sympathetic, but troubled. "And it's also possible he made a mistake. That he thought he was updating the discs, but pushed the wrong keys. Accidentally copying the story again and again."

"I don't like to think of that," Abbie said unhappily. "It's too painful. He was... He'd been such a *bright* man in his time."

"My one hope is this," Yates said gruffly. He gave the computer's side an unaffectionate pat. "I found one disc apart from the others. In the back of a drawer. It's labeled Inventory and dated eighteen months ago. But I can't get into it. I need some kind of password to access it. It must be some kind of LOKFILE system.

"I've tried everything," he muttered. "Every relevant word I can think of—collection, inventory, coins, stamps, his name, your name, everybody in the family's name. I even tried Bucky. Nothing. I can't get in."

Abbie straightened her back and looked at the computer as if it were a faithless friend. "It could be any one of a million words. It could be anything."

"Exactly." Yates took off his glasses and rubbed his eyes. "And you said you haven't any idea. None?"

"None," she repeated. She glanced at him with concern. He was probably much tireder than he'd admit. But he still looked immaculate, even if he did smell faintly of the pleasant scents of horse and straw.

She had a sudden illogical impulse to reach over and loosen his tie, unbutton the collar of his shirt, muss his hair and tell him to relax.

At that moment he raised his eyes and met hers. Abbie's breath stuck in her throat, and she found she could not turn away. His deep-set eyes were the darkest she'd ever seen, the lashes thick and black. His eyebrows were as dark as jet.

She smiled nervously, a tiny smile that was not much more than a quiver at the edges of her lips. Like a thunderbolt his gaze fell to her mouth, and only then did she regain the power to turn away from him.

Out of the corner of her eye, she saw him put on his glasses again, tighten his tie and flick an invisible piece of lint from his trouser leg. Then he adjusted his hearing aid.

"Ah, yes," he said brusquely. "Where were we? I was...woolgathering for a moment."

Abbie trained her gaze on the computer screen. Her heart seemed afflicted with a strange case of the shakes, and she didn't know why. She and Yates had stared at each other for only an instant—that was all.

"This disc," she said, nodding at the screen. "We need a password, and we haven't got one. So now what?"

He rose again and resumed his pacing. He reminded her of a panther measuring the limits of its cage. But that was absurd, she told herself, because he wasn't pantherlike at all. He was harmless, repressed, mild, actually more brotherly than any of her brothers.

But when he stopped pacing and looked at her, instinctively she looked away, as if his bespectacled gaze might cast a spell over her.

"What we may have to do," he said, "is inventory these collections from scratch. I can't find any recent written records, either, to work from. This disc is it."

He walked to the table and opened a manila folder. In it were pages filled with lists of passwords he had tried to access the disc. He pushed it in front of Abbie. When he did so, his arm accidentally brushed her shoulder, sending a shiver through her.

Her body tensed. Why was she so damnably *aware* of this man? Now he stood behind her, and she could feel his nearness.

"Your father said most of the written records got thrown out." His voice was nearly toneless, but it still sent a minute frisson up her spine.

She nodded, feeling more ill at ease than before. The matter of the written records hadn't seemed important until now. Everyone had believed the discs held all the recent inventories needed. But no one had ever checked.

"When Grandpa died," she said slowly, "this office was a mess. He'd stopped throwing out newspapers, magazines, even advertisements. There were papers everywhere. We all pitched in to clean it up."

"Who's 'we'?" Yates asked. He sat down beside her again. His expression, his movements were casual, almost cultivatedly so.

Abbie drew a deep breath. "All of us," she said. "Daddy. My brothers. Me. And Lucky—even he helped. He came as soon as he heard about Grandpa. They were close. Lucky was interested in coins, too. He was a big help."

"I can imagine."

She darted an uneasy glance his way. Had she detected sarcasm in his voice? But his face was innocent, the line of his mouth guileless. She turned her eyes from him and stared, instead, at the pages filled with the failed passwords. She sighed and made a face of exasperation. "Oh, this is impossible. Why don't we just start going through the coins? Then the stamps. We'll probably end up doing it, anyway."

He shook his head. "Only as a last resort. I need an inventory. I might miss something. How can I tell if everything's there unless I have a list of everything that's *supposed* to be there?"

She nodded in unhappy agreement.

"Like I said, this disc is my last hope. But it's better than nothing."

"Not much," she said.

He smiled at her, a slow, teasing, slightly crooked smile. "We'll do it. I've got a hunch."

She smiled back, shyness mixing with ruefulness. "Why? Do you think we make a good pair?"

She could have bitten her tongue as soon as she said the words. In confusion she looked at the wall clock. She pushed her chair away from the library table and rose as quickly as she could. "Omigosh," she muttered. "It's almost one o'clock—time to feed Frosty."

He, too, had risen, and when she started for the door she found him squarely blocking her path. "I'll help you."

She shook her head. "No. Thank you."

"He's starting to stand. But he needs support. You're dealing with sixty-plus pounds of horse. You need help."

"I'm strong. I've fed foals before." She started to skirt around Yates. He put out his hand as if to stop her. She almost dodged him, but he caught her gently but firmly by the elbow.

His touch swept through her in a fiery surge. She stared up at him in alarm. For a second all mildness vanished from his face. But then, as if he willed his expression to change, he gave her an apologetic smile that made the corner of his mouth twitch. He let go of her arm, adjusted his glasses and straightened his tie.

"Sorry," he said. "I didn't mean to...get personal. It won't happen again."

"Good," she breathed.

But she didn't move away. They stood like two combatants, each tensed, each wary of the other.

Both were breathing harder than they should have been. Both were startled by the ring of the phone. Abbie felt as if she had been under some uncomfortable enchantment, but suddenly it was broken.

Yates stepped aside and she hurried to the living room to pick up the phone. "Hello?" she said, gripping the receiver tightly. Her voice shook slightly.

"Lucky!" she cried, and her face broke into a tense smile. She saw Yates standing by the door, watching her, his arms crossed. Her smile stiffened as she listened to Lucky's lazy drawl.

"I love you, too," she replied. But her eyes were locked with Yates's when she said the words.

She turned away so she wouldn't see him. She squeezed her eyes shut and pictured Lucky's handsome blue-eyed face.

"I love you very much," she told Lucky. Her voice was fervent, as earnest as a woman in prayer.

I do love him, she thought. *With all my heart. And I would never betray him or lie to him in any way, because that's the worst thing one human being can do to another. I will be faithful to him forever.*

CHAPTER FIVE

SHE KEPT HER BACK to Yates. "Where are you?" she asked Lucky anxiously. "How are you? Is there any chance you'll be here for Christmas?"

"Not much, honey," Lucky drawled. "I'm in Hawaii."

The room seemed to close in on Abbie, smothering her. What was Lucky doing half a world away?

"Hawaii?" she asked, her voice full of disbelief.

"It was an offer I couldn't refuse. There's a new rodeo in Honolulu."

"But you said you'd be on the coast..."

"Bigger money at stake here, sugar."

"But Hawaii? How'd you get to *Hawaii?*"

"There's this good old boy, a *paniola,* who was rode-oin' on the West Coast."

Abbie's face was rigid with unhappiness. Lucky's words barely made sense to her. But she tried to sound calm, rational. "What's a *paniola?*"

"A Hawaiian cowboy, sugar baby. That's what they call 'em. He works for a rich guy on Maui. Guy sent a private plane for him—told him to bring the best talent he could find to upgrade the competition. Especially in bull ridin'. 'Bring the best,' he said. Guess I don't hafta tell you who that is."

"But—"

''This guy's payin' for *everything*. Hotel's right on the beach. I'm sittin' on one of them Hawaiian balconies right now, lookin' at the ocean.''

He didn't say he wished she was there. He didn't even say he missed her. But she tried to understand. With Lucky she always tried to understand.

''It... it sounds wonderful,'' she managed to say.

''This is the life. Lord, if those jerks back in reform school could see me. All the people that told me I'd never amount to nothin'. For the first time in my life I feel like I've arrived. And I'm gonna come back with money in my pockets. You're gonna be proud of me—wait and see.''

Abbie swallowed hard. Lucky's youth had been so filled with humiliations that achievement meant the world to him. He sounded as excited as a child, and why shouldn't he? He'd never had a real childhood. She should be glad he was happy. And he *was* there to work, to win money for their future. What difference did it make if that work was in California or Hawaii?

But then Abbie thought she heard a woman giggle in the background. She didn't want to be suspicious or jealous, but she winced. ''How will you get back?''

''He's flyin' us back. But I gotta stay over the holidays. I mean, he's callin' the shots. Ain't nothin' I can do about it.''

''Lucky, a lot of things have happened here—''

''What's the temperature there?''

''About ten above zero, I guess. What's that got to do—''

''It's eighty-nine here,'' Lucky said with satisfaction. ''Palm trees. Blue water. Flowers everywhere.''

''A lot of things have happened here. Sprint had a colt—''

''Ol' Sprint? At this time of year?''

He laughed. Abbie set her teeth. "It nearly died."

"Probably better off dead, sugar."

Abbie sucked in her breath as if she'd been struck. Couldn't he stop basking in his own contentment long enough just to *listen?* "There's more," she said. "A man came to the ranch. He's here to—"

There were sounds of a scuffle on the other end of the line. She heard Lucky's voice, muffled, as if he was holding his hand over the receiver. "Stop that!" she thought he said, and "Hey!"

"Lucky?"

"Yeah, yeah. What?"

"I said—"

The scuffling sounds started again. Lucky seemed to be suppressing laughter. "I've got to get off, hon. This connection's no good."

"Where *are* you?" she asked, her patience wearing thin. "Which hotel? If I need to get in touch...?"

"Baby, I can't hear you. See you sometime after New Year's. I'm gonna bring you such presents, sugar. You're gonna love 'em, I promise."

He hung up. Abbie stood, clenching the receiver. Then she slammed it hard enough to shake the phone table. She was breathing fast.

Her father's voice, edged with displeasure, startled her. "So, Lucky's in Hawaii? How nice—for him."

Abbie wheeled and saw Frazier looming in the kitchen doorway. Bundled into his heaviest jacket, his figure was bearlike.

His face was reddened with cold, his shoulders slumped with obvious fatigue. From the knees down, his jeans were wet and icy, and his boots looked waterlogged.

When he stripped off his gloves, the knuckles of both hands were cracked and bleeding. Although Frazier had put Abbie on the defensive, she stared at his raw knuckles with a surge of sympathy impossible to repress. Every winter the long hours in the cold made her father's hands crack and bleed.

"Wish *I* was in Hawaii," Frazier said, unknotting the muffler and taking off his hat. "Yessir," he said, his eyes holding hers as he blew on his damaged knuckles. "I wish I was sittin' in Hawaii."

She drew herself up. Yates, she thanked heaven, had disappeared; he was probably hovering over his precious computer.

"You should stop working when your hands get that way," she said, keeping emotion out of her voice.

"I've got no choice. I've got to work if this ranch is going to stay in business. I'm not like Lucky."

"Lucky works," she said stubbornly. "He works almost every day of the year. He just happens to be doing it in Hawaii."

Frazier gave a snort of bitter laughter. "Yeah. He works for eight seconds a night—if he doesn't get thrown on his head. Riding *bulls*. Now there's a vocation for a man with brains. A great future, riding bulls."

He stripped off one sodden boot and a wet sock. His foot, unlike his hands, was not red but sinisterly pale, as if blood had stopped flowing to it.

"What did you do?" Abbie demanded in consternation. "Fall in the water? You're soaked. You'll get frostbite. Or pneumonia. You should go soak that foot."

"Yeah," Frazier said, grimacing as he pulled off his other boot. "I fell. Mingus and I were swinging picks trying to keep that blankety-blank water hole open and I slipped. It was good I didn't go in deeper than I did. Got to get back to it. Mingus is out there alone."

He pulled off his sock and tried to wriggle his toes, which looked gray and shriveled. His face twisted in pain.

Suddenly Abbie wanted to cry, both over Lucky's defection and her father's suffering. Instead, she held herself straighter. "Take a bath and get into dry clothes. I'll fix you something to eat."

He shrugged out of his coat and rose heavily from his chair. "I'll fix my own food. It's time for you to tend that swaybacked excuse for a horse you got on my porch."

Abbie looked at her father with concern. He seemed unsteady on his numbed feet, and he looked every one of his fifty-nine years. Suddenly she understood that it was true: he was getting too old and tired for this life.

"The colt can wait," she said. "I'll make coffee."

She headed purposefully for the kitchen, but his hand shot out, grasping her shoulder. Wordlessly, he turned her to face him.

"Abbie, I can do it myself. You really want to do something for me? 'Cause I don't want any coffee from you, no soup, nothing like that."

He stared down at her. The weather-hardened lines of his face deepened, but his eyes were kind. "Best thing you could do for me is face facts about Lucky. That boy is flat no good, honey. Never has been, never will be."

Abbie tossed her head in frustration. "Don't worry about me. Worry about keeping the water open. Worry about your hands. Worry about the cattle. I'm fine."

Frazier bent closer, a look akin to sorrow on his face. "Abbie, I can't stand the way he treats you—"

"He treats me like an equal," Abbie interrupted, defiant. "He treats me like an adult. I don't need moonlight and roses. I'm a woman, not a child. I don't have to have him here every minute to know he's faithful."

The frown line between Frazier's shaggy brows grew deeper. "How do you know he's faithful? He's away from you probably 340 days a year. You're a nice girl, too soft-hearted for your own good. But he's a sorry piece of trash. And that's the truth."

"Don't say that!" Abbie retorted with passion. "You don't know how hard he's worked, how far he's come. Oh, maybe his manners aren't fine enough for you, but who did he ever have to teach him?"

She reached deep inside herself, to the part of her soul that always stood up for the underdog. "This Hawaii trip—" she held her chin high "—just shows how well he's done for himself."

Frazier shook his head. "For himself. But not for you. Oh, he could always make you laugh. And he sucked up to your grandpa something shameless. But he's a selfish little—"

"Don't talk like that," Abbie ordered. "Don't."

"How can you defend him? He's not even coming to see you at Christmas."

"Why should he?" Abbie shot back. "When you treat him like dirt. Grandpa was the only man in this family who was nice to him—the only one. Why shouldn't he go where people treat him as if he's important? Treat him as if he's human."

Frazier sighed, shaking his head. "Abbie, you're the stubbornest woman that ever walked the earth. Can't you admit—"

With a twisting movement, she broke away from him. "I'll set out the antiseptic and salve," she said.

She stalked toward the bathroom, her emotions warring. If she hadn't convinced Frazier with her arguments, she had at least convinced herself. Why should Lucky spend Christmas in Nebraska, being snubbed by her father? Why shouldn't he go to a warm beautiful place where he could win prize money? *And* be appreciated.

Even though Lucky had hurt her, she would not be disloyal to him. People truly in love were never disloyal. Not in the slightest.

And Abbie, believing herself truly in love, was loyal to a fault.

Her emotions still roiling, she fed Frosty. Frazier left to rejoin Mingus. Yates stayed in the office, working. Abbie was about to rejoin him when the phone rang again.

Perhaps, she thought with a surge of hope, it was Lucky, calling to make amends for their conversation being cut short.

But it was not Lucky. It was her oldest brother, John.

"John, you just missed Daddy. He's out with Mingus."

"Abbie . . . I've got some bad news. We can't make it home for Christmas."

Abbie's heart pitched so sharply it hurt. "Not home? John, it's our last Christmas at SkyRim. You've got to come. We've *never* had Christmas without you. It won't *be* Christmas without you."

"Ab, there's no help for it. Sandy's pregnant. We didn't plan it, we didn't expect it, but it happened, and we're happy. But she's having a tough time. The doctor says she shouldn't travel."

John—a father at last? Abbie could hardly believe it. He and Sandy wanted children, but on a teacher's salary, they kept postponing. She was elated for them, but devastated for herself. She'd counted on being reunited with her brother and sister-in-law. John had always been her most sympathetic brother, Sandy the sister-in-law to whom she felt closest. She immediately felt guilty for being selfish.

"I ... Congratulations," she managed to say. "I mean that. A baby couldn't have better parents. This is wonderful."

"Look, Ab, I can't run up a big phone bill. Tell Dad, will you? We can't make it, but we'll be there with you in spirit—okay?"

"Of course. He'll be so happy. Oh, he won't *say* anything, but inwardly he'll be busting his buttons."

"Listen," John said, hesitation in his voice, "I'm sorry we're not getting home, mainly because of ... well, you. I know you haven't been happy with any of us lately. Because of selling SkyRim and all."

Abbie felt another surge of guilt, deeper and darker. She was sick to death of disagreements and discord. She wanted this last Christmas at the ranch to be a time of reconciliation, of togetherness and peace.

"You all know how I feel about selling the ranch," she said. "I don't mean to make trouble. It's just that—"

"No," John said, interrupting her. "You don't have to explain. It gives me some sad feelings, too. But you've got to understand, Abbie. Dad's getting too old for this. He's so closemouthed, he'd never say it, but he's *got* to take it easier. He's having blood-pressure problems. Serious ones. If he doesn't slow down, he's going to have a stroke one of these days."

"Blood pressure? Why didn't anybody tell me?"

"He didn't want you to worry, that's why. You're the family worrywart. *I* wouldn't know if Preston hadn't found out. Last time Preston was home, he saw the medication in the medicine cabinet. He knew what it was. He cornered Dad, made him admit it."

At first she hadn't wanted to believe John, but now a chilling certainty gripped her. Preston was a medical student. He understood such things.

"Now don't go into shock on me," John said. "Nothing bad has happened to him—yet. I was going to tell you this in person—it would have been better. I want you to understand that he's got to sell the ranch for his own good. There's more than money at stake here, Abbie."

She swallowed hard. "Everybody knew this except me? You *all* knew—"

"I was going to tell you, Abbie. I didn't think it was right, your not knowing. But Preston thought it would be easier if we were all there, and we could get everything out into the open and... Well, it's not working out that way."

"Didn't Daddy think I was mature enough? I mean, this puts a new light on everything."

"Look, you're the baby of the family. You're the only girl. You know Dad—he doesn't want anybody feeling sorry for him. Let alone a *woman.*"

Abbie nodded unhappily. "That's Daddy, all right."

"And frankly, he's worried about you. We all are. It's that damn Lucky Gibbs."

Abbie's emotions veered from sadness to resentment. "John, don't you start on him, too."

"I'm not starting. I've felt that way all along."

"No. I won't talk about it. I was glad everybody was coming home because we need to talk about the ranch. I don't *want* to be at odds with everybody else. I hate it. Because I love you all."

"Now, Abbie, don't get mushy. I'm trying to have a serious discussion with you. I'm doing my best."

"Well, can't I even say I love you? I do. Nobody in this family can ever talk about feelings. *Nobody.*"

"Just because we don't talk about them doesn't mean we don't have them. And you're changing the subject. I was talking about Lucky—"

"John, don't. *Please.* You don't understand him, that's all. He puts up a facade, but underneath he's very—"

"Abbie, I shouldn't say this, but you're riding for a fall with this guy. He's told you so many sob stories you'd defend him no matter what."

"John, no more discussion. None. If you can't come for Christmas, don't make it worse by giving me lectures. Can't you do that much?"

He was silent. Then she heard him sigh. "All right. But about the other, about the ranch—is it easier for you to understand now?"

Her resentment melted. Sadness and resignation replaced it. "I understand. I just wish you'd told me sooner."

"So do I, kid. So do I. But like I say, you know Dad."

"Yes. I know."

"Listen, Abbie, I'll call again Christmas Day. I'm sorry we won't be there. I'll...kind of miss getting the tree with you."

She bit the inside of her cheek. "I'll miss you and Sandy, too. But it's a wonderful reason to have to stay home. Congratulations again."

"Thanks, Ab."

He said goodbye and hung up. Abbie hung up, too, then stood staring at the phone. How like her father not to say he was having health problems. She'd been so concerned about her grandfather's health, it had never occurred to her to worry about her father's.

She was ashamed of having argued with Frazier and adding to his burdens. And she hadn't done anything about getting ready for Christmas. She and John and her grandfather had always gone together to cut down a tree. And she and John had always decorated it. She could not remember a time when they had not.

Well, the other brothers would be here with their wives, and her two nephews would come, too. She would get the tree by herself. And she would try to be more considerate of her father.

Then, if he would only be tolerant enough not to criticize Lucky all the time, perhaps—just perhaps—this Christmas would be a pleasure, a time of warmth and acceptance, and not a trial.

She started bundling herself into her winter jacket. Yates wandered out of the office and into the kitchen to refill his coffee cup. One dark brow rose in question as he looked her up and down. "Where are you going?"

"Out," she said, turning from his stare. Why did he make her feel *guilty?* As if she was being unfaithful to Lucky simply by being near him? It made no sense.

"I can see that. Why?"

"To get a Christmas tree," she said crisply. "My brother and grandfather and I used to do it together. My brother just called. He can't come. I'll do it myself."

"Alone?"

"Yes."

He gave her a slight one-cornered smile. "It's going to be a mighty small tree, if you're the one chopping and hauling."

"No, it's not," she said, rebellion flashing in her eyes. "I've got one picked out. It's big. Taller than you, even."

His smile stayed sardonic. "I think I'd better go with you."

"I don't need any help," Abbie said with conviction.

"No? I do. I need a break from that damn computer."

She shrugged as if she didn't care what he needed or didn't.

"Any of your brothers about my size? Have any old clothes lying around?"

She glanced at him as impersonally as possible. "John," she said. "His room's the last one on the left. I'll be in the barn."

"The barn?"

"There's an old-fashioned sleigh. It's what we always use. I'll hitch up the horse. Hurry up, because I won't wait on you. I have to be back in two hours to feed Frosty."

He pushed his glasses up higher, to the bridge of his nose. He raised his eyebrows a fraction of an inch higher, giving his expression an even more mocking cast. "Yes, ma'am," he said.

She turned and left him there. *Let him smirk,* she thought, glad to escape him. *I'll have the horse harnessed and be out of here before he remembers which way a cowboy hat points. He'll probably be the only man in Nebraska putting boots on over silk socks.*

She was taken aback when he joined her before she had old Sprint even half-harnessed. She had always had help before when she did the job, and even then, did it only once a year. Her unpracticed fingers were making long work of the job. She was further distracted by one of the barn cats, which kept rubbing against her ankles.

Then Yates appeared, nodded, and wordlessly began to help her, working on Sprint's opposite side.

"I can do it myself," she protested. "My grandfather taught me how."

"So did mine," he said without rancor, working faster and more surely than she did.

She labored at fastening a particularly stubborn buckle and tried not to look at him. A change of clothing had altered him—startlingly.

John's old red jacket stretched tightly across his shoulders, emphasizing their width. John's faded jeans made his legs look longer and revealed their muscularity. John's boots, scuffed and well-worn, made him tower yet another inch and a half above her. And John's dark Stetson hat, pulled down low over his eyes, brought out the strong line of his jaw, the stubborn jut of his chin.

Only the glasses and hearing aid looked out of place. That, and the fact he hadn't been able to find good gloves. The ones he wore were of cloth and had holes at the fingertips. He didn't seem to notice. He seemed just as natural, perhaps even more so, in the cast-off ranch clothes as he did in his city ones.

He finished buckling the harness on his side and moved next to Abbie, helping her. "This, I take it," he said, glancing at Sprint, "is the not-so-proud mother. Lord, he's going to look just like her—swayback and all."

"I like her—swayback and all."

"Why?"

They both reached for the same buckle, the last one, their gloved fingers brushing. Swiftly she withdrew her hand, letting him insert the buckle's tongue and draw the leather strap tight.

She patted the old mare's shoulder. "This was my mother's horse. I know Sprint doesn't seem like much, but..." Abbie's voice trailed off, for she was incapable of explaining exactly what the old horse, despite its lack of beauty, meant to her.

He nodded curtly as if he understood. "I see. Can you drive this thing? Or do you want me to?"

She gave him a furtive look. He seemed perfectly confident about driving the sleigh. She shook her head. "I can do it. I've done it for years. It's just that old-fashioned harness—I'd never done that alone. But Grandpa had me driving by the time I was twelve."

Suddenly she realized that this was the last time she would ever harness Sprint at SkyRim. Regret, mixed with longing, overwhelmed her.

She couldn't sell Sprint, or Frosty, either—she was bonding far too closely with the little colt to part with him. Or her own horse, Shawnee. But what would become of them?

Her father would let her keep them, she knew, but she would have to board them somewhere, live apart from them, trapped in town. The thought made her so sad she was almost physically ill with it.

"What's the matter?" Yates said, frowning. "You look pale. Are you all right?"

"Yes," Abbie lied. But she knew that until this moment, she had never admitted to herself how absolutely terrible it was going to be to leave SkyRim forever. She resisted the urge to bury her face against Sprint's dappled hide and weep.

Instead, she squared her shoulders and tossed her head. "Let's go," she said brusquely, and cursed the fates for allowing this emotion to strike her full force when the man at her side was Connley, not Lucky.

Lucky would have understood. Lucky would have told her everything would be all right.

YATES CONNLEY just stared down at her, his expression unreadable.

She drove as Yates expected she would—well—her hands light and sure on the reins.

In the back of the sleigh she'd put an ax so old and heavy it looked as if Abe Lincoln might have used it to split rails. How she expected to wield such a thing, he didn't know.

She was silent during the ride. The old mare had a surprisingly swift trot, and the sleigh skimmed over snow just as smoothly as he remembered his grandfather's doing years ago.

He pretended to watch the flat land turn to rolling land, then ascend more sharply uphill. But the scenery caught his attention only slightly. It was Abbie who interested him, and covertly he watched her.

She wore a bulky sage green jacket and a darker green Western hat. She'd pinned her gold hair back with a barrette so that it fluttered down her back, shooting off glints of gold.

Her profile seemed solemn to him, in spite of her pert nose. He thought he could see emotions changing on her face even as the country they drove through changed. It was as if he could actually witness how tumultuous her feelings were.

Maybe, he thought, the truth was sinking in at last about Gibbs. He hoped so.

She drove the sleigh to the top of the bluff. The only sounds were the soft sigh of the wind, the creak of the leather harness and the muffled thuds of the mare's hooves. If the sleigh had ever had bells, they were long since rusted and gone.

He was oddly surprised by the view when they reached the crest of their ascent.

"This is it," Abbie said, her voice flat with repressed emotion. She nodded and got out, as if the view didn't interest her. But then she paused and stood staring out across the river and at the plain beyond. She took in the scene as if transfixed by it, held in thrall.

His gaze followed hers. He was not a man given to nostalgia. But the view along this river, the Platte, reminded him of another vista along another river, the Missouri.

He remembered his grandfather taking him along a high, wild green bluff where there was no path. The land was not his grandfather's; it belonged to a stranger.

That land had been too forested for animals to graze and too steep to till. It wasn't good for much of anything except scenery, his grandfather had said, but it did have one secret, one he'd wished to share with Yates.

The old man had led him to an ancient juniper tree in a sheltered niche of the bluff. Standing there and looking out, Yates could see the wild brown Missouri foaming below him. Beyond it stretched the land.

He had always struggled, even as a child, to keep his emotions at bay, but the sight had stirred him. He'd tried to keep it from showing on his face.

Then his grandfather told Yates why he'd brought him there. The old man's own grandmother was buried there, her grave unmarked beneath the gnarled juniper. The idea of a dead woman, an ancestor, hidden in such a dramatic place had startled the boy.

"My grandparents wintered here when they came from Ireland," the old man had said. "They crossed the river, heading West. But my grandmother turned sick. With child, she was. That child was my father, your great-grandfather. She died giving him life. In the darkest part of December, that brave woman brought forth life."

Yates had stood staring at that unmarked grave beneath the juniper tree. He would never have guessed it held a grave, had his grandfather not told him. He tried to imagine that long-ago woman, so far from her home, dying on a strange frontier. The idea troubled him.

The old man had put his hand on Yates's shoulder. "She said to my grandfather, 'Bury me up on that bluff, where the view's so pretty. They say when you cross that river, you've reached the West. Well, I crossed that river. I came that far. I'm proud to have come that far.' "

Yates's grandfather had shaken his head. "She should have been proud. And he honored her wishes. But there was no proper cemetery here, and he didn't mark the grave. Someone might have disturbed it. Nobody knows it's here—except family. Me, your grandmother, your father. Now you."

Yates had been old enough to understand his grandfather was passing something important on to him, something the old man considered almost momentous.

"My grandfather married a widder-woman and headed West again. He needed a mother for that baby, she needed a husband. She had a little girl of her own, but three years old."

The old man's hand had tightened on his shoulder. "He made it West. Outlived that wife, too. Married a third, a pretty woman, a nice woman, part Shoshone. I remember her well."

The old man had paused a moment. "But it's the blood of that woman there," he'd said, nodding at the earth, "that's in your veins and mine. Pioneer blood. Remember that. Always remember that. Someday you'll show your own sons this place."

Now Yates shook his head as if to clear it. He did not often remember what his grandfather had said or think of that lonely grave. In fact, he tried not to think of it at all. The rest of his family was gone now. As far as he knew, he was the only person alive who knew where that grave was.

He felt Abbie giving him a sidelong look. The expression on her face was partly shy, partly speculative.

"Why are you standing there staring out at the river like that?" she asked.

"I . . . was thinking," he said, frowning. He turned his back to the river so he wouldn't see it anymore. "What were you doing? You're pretty quiet yourself."

She put her hands in her pockets. "Thinking, too," she said. The wind fluttered her long hair.

"Yes," he said, rubbing his hands together briskly to warm them. "Well. You have a tree picked out?"

"Yes. That one." She nodded at a surprisingly full cedar tree almost seven feet tall. It was a strong healthy tree, not at all like the twisted juniper at the grave site. But now, reawakened, the memory of that pioneer grave wouldn't go away.

Wordlessly he took the ax from the back of the sleigh. He concentrated all his restless energy and focused his maverick thoughts on getting the tree down as quickly and cleanly as possible.

When he'd lived on the ranch, he'd liked using an ax. Chopping wood was the best release for tension he'd ever found. Chopping wood or riding a horse at full gallop— but he hadn't ridden a horse for years, although he'd been good at it.

He aimed his strokes with such accuracy and struck with such force that the tree came down in a remarkably short time. It swayed, then fell to the snow with a cracking sound. With one last stroke, he severed the strip of bark holding it in place. The tangy smell of resin filled the cold air.

He hauled it to the sleigh and half lifted, half hurled it to the sleigh bed. "You'd never have managed it by yourself," he grumbled to Abbie.

She stared at him with such a stricken look that he was startled. Behind her stretched the vista of river and plains.

"What's wrong now?" he demanded. Had he hurt her feelings? Her damned emotions were throwing his own out of kilter, as if too much feeling was somehow contagious.

"I don't know," she said with a helpless gesture. "It's such a beautiful tree. It seems a shame to cut it down. Maybe we should've—I should've let it stand. It could've stayed here where it belongs."

"A tree's a tree," he said, jerking his hat brim down lower. "You wanted one, you got one. Let's go. You've got a horse to feed. I've got a computer to hate."

She climbed into the sleigh and took up the reins. "Why do you do it if you hate it?" she asked, almost warily. "You looked so...intense, but so at *home* cutting down that tree. Sometimes...well, you puzzle me. You don't seem as if you should sit all day staring at a computer. You said you grew up on a ranch..."

She shook her head as if she didn't understand, flicked the reins and coaxed the mare back toward the ranch.

Moodily, he watched her profile. She still looked so sad it unsettled something deep within him. He didn't recognize the feeling, and he didn't like it. "It's a hard life, ranching," he said.

She sighed, her face growing even more somber. "Yes," she said. "Hard." The words seemed freighted with unhappiness.

He stopped looking at her. He watched the sweep of the snowy land, instead. "He—your father—said he's giving up the ranch. But you don't like the idea."

She lifted one shoulder in a shrug he supposed was meant to look careless. Instead, it struck him as pained but resigned. "My brother said my father has health problems. Blood pressure. I didn't know that. I knew the ranch wasn't making money, but..." She fell silent.

"You understand, then?" he persisted. "Why he feels he has to quit?"

She held herself straighter, but her jaw gave a frustrated little jerk. "I understand. He's been at it all his life. And it never gets easier. It just gets harder. I'm learning to accept it. It would be selfish for me not to. But I wish he didn't have to. That's all."

She glanced at the sky. It had grown darker while they were on the bluff. The wind had risen, as well.

"Now a blizzard's supposed to come, a bad one," she said. "That's the trouble with ranching, Grandpa used to say. You have to take whatever that wide Nebraska sky throws at you."

Expertly she flicked the reins again. Yates regarded her over the rims of his glasses, liking her efficient grace. He was getting to like it too much, so he tried to force himself to ignore it.

"Yeah," he said, squinting upward himself. "My granddad used to say pretty much the same."

She cast him a measuring look. "You said he ranched. And you spent time there. A lot?"

He sidestepped the question. Too often, since the Claridge case, it seemed the best days of his life had been spent there, but they were long ago and over. Things had been simpler then. Demanding, but simpler. "Some."

"How much?"

"Eight years. From the time I was nine until I was seventeen."

She looked at him, surprised, as if she couldn't quite believe him. "Years? Why?"

"My mother died."

She turned her attention back to the trotting mare. "Oh. I'm sorry."

"It was a long time ago."

"So you were glad to leave it finally—the ranch, I mean? It wasn't your style, I guess."

He didn't like delving back into memories. He didn't deal much with his distant past—what good did it do? "Let's not talk about my style," he said. "Let's talk about yours. What'll you do when you leave here?"

She raised her chin slightly. "I don't know," she said, "I've spent my whole life here."

Her honesty made him feel another tug of reluctant sympathy. "Listen," his tone became more earnest. "It doesn't sound as if your father has much choice."

"I know." She kept her eyes on the horizon. The empty plains and gathering clouds stretched out until they met in a straight line. "It's just that I love it—the land, the space, this big old sky. No matter what it throws at us."

He saw tears glitter in her eyes, but she forced them back. She lifted her chin higher. "Well, maybe I'm a vanishing breed, but I'm not vanished yet. It's not the end of the world. Lucky and I'll have a place of our own one of these days. It's not like I'm leaving this life forever."

A vise seemed to clamp, tight and cold, on Yates's heart. She really had no chance of happiness, because she was right, dammit. She was made for a kind of life that was vanishing. What did she have left, except her blind faith in Lucky Gibbs?

And that faith was going to die. He himself would kill it. And he would lie to her up to the moment he did it. Well, it was his job, he rationalized. A good undercover cop had to lie and do it well. He'd been at it so long it had become second nature to say things he did not mean, to project emotions he did not feel. Hypocrisy, for the sake of justice, had become natural to him.

So, like the expert hypocrite he was, when they returned to the ranch, he helped her unhitch the sleigh, rub down the mare and carry the fragrant tree into the house as if he really gave a damn about her having a happy Christmas.

Merry Christmas, Abbie, he thought grimly as he wrestled her tree through the door. *Peace on Earth and death to dreams.*

CHAPTER SIX

ABBIE DECORATED the tree, but not the rest of the house. Her brother Preston, always the first one home, would join her in that job. He and she had done it together since they were children. Now that he was married, his wife helped, too. It was part of the tradition.

But family tradition was drawing to an end, she thought, as she set the star atop the tree, the finishing touch. She tried not to think about it.

She took care of the colt. She sat at Yates's side in the office as he frowned over the computer and tried password after password without success.

She didn't hear from her father or Mingus. Heaven only knew what problem they might encounter out on the range. She tried not to dwell on that, either, especially now that she knew her father was not as well as he should be.

After Frosty's afternoon feeding, she bundled up to go to the barn to turn out the horses and clean their stalls. She could do that much for her father. Besides, she was restless and eager for an excuse to get out of the house.

Yates insisted on helping. He wasn't getting anywhere, he grumbled. Another stint of physical labor might clear his mind. Abbie couldn't keep him from donning John's jacket and hat and boots again and plodding with her to the barn. He seemed even more restless than she.

There was work to be done; hard unpleasant work, but Yates labored without complaint. He was as efficient at mucking out a stable as he was at everything else. He wielded an expert pitchfork, and Abbie could not help but be grateful to him.

The temperature dropped ominously even as they worked. Reluctantly Abbie led the horses back into their stalls; they were mettlesome for want of exercise.

Her father's horse, a big bay gelding, stamped and half reared, threatening to kick. Yates seized it by the mane and forced the animal into its stall. Abbie was puzzled. How could a man show such mastery with an animal, yet be so bland, so tame, with people?

She did not have time to wonder further. As they trudged back to the ranch house, the wind rose, as sharp, frigid and savage as if it had rushed directly from the North Pole. Needles of sleet began to swirl down.

"Blizzard," Abbie muttered unhappily, ducking her head so that the wind didn't slap her face so harshly.

"I hope your father and that Mingus character don't get caught in this," Yates said from between clenched teeth. "It's going to be a bad one."

As if to prove the truth of what he said, the wind gathered itself into such a violent blast that Abbie staggered at its force.

Yates seized her and drew her to him to steady her. She huddled against him to escape the cold's assault. The sleet turned to snow, and his arm tightened around her, steering her through its blinding sweep.

"Oh!" was all she could manage to say when they finally reached the safety of the house. She stamped her feet and clapped her hands, trying to restore the feeling. Suddenly she realized Yates's arm was still around her.

She went motionless and looked up at him. His glasses were steamed up, and his face was darkened with cold. She had an absurd urge to strip off her gloves and place her hands on his cheeks to warm him.

He kept his arm in place. Over the rims of his clouded glasses, he stared down at her. The melting snow glistened on the brim of his hat.

Abbie's heart took an odd skip that left her feeling empty and breathless. His face bent nearer to hers, his lips parting slightly.

She found that she was raising her face to his and that her own lips were parting, as if she was about to say something to him.

But she could think of nothing to say. She felt lost in the depths of his intense black eyes. His arm tightened around her possessively, drawing her nearer to him. His mouth descended another fraction of an inch.

Then, as if both jolted simultaneously by the same shock of electricity, they blinked and looked away from each other. Abbie drew in her breath sharply, startled and embarrassed. His arm fell away from her shoulders. He stepped back, and so did she.

He straightened his glasses, then shook his head. He took off his ragged gloves and examined them with great concentration.

"It's cold out there," he said. It was a totally unnecessary statement.

"Yes." Her comment was as needless as his, but it seemed important to say something, say anything. It was as if words, even gratuitous ones, would erase the strangeness of the moment. "Yes, it is," she said.

He turned away, undoing John's old red jacket. "You should take a shower," he said. "Get the blood circulating. You look frozen."

She tried to focus her attention on peeling off her gloves. "So do you. You go first."

THE MAN WHO CAME FOR CHRISTMAS   101

He shrugged out of the jacket and hung it on the coat tree by the door. "No. I've had one. You go."

He didn't look at her; instead, he moved his shoulders restlessly and turned toward her grandfather's study. "I'll get the computer fired up." He pulled off his glasses and blew on the lenses to clear them.

She watched him stride into the other room, her heart beating crazily.

It's because I miss Lucky, she told herself. *I turned to him like that because I wished he was Lucky, that's all.*

Abbie grew worried about her father. Night was falling, and outside, the blizzard filled the air with snow. Where *was* Frazier? How was he? Why didn't he come home?

MINGUS FINALLY appeared at the kitchen door at about five-thirty, just after she'd fed Frosty and given him his shot. The foreman was so caked with snow he refused to come inside. Even his eyebrows were white with it. And he was alone, which alarmed Abbie.

"That old flatbed we use to haul the hay, she done give up the ghost," Mingus explained, stamping his feet. "She come loose, slip half into the creek bed, break an axle. Her deck fold up like cardboard. She out on the far river forty, goin' nowhere. Your pa, he drove the tractor over to Hurleys' place—see about borrowin' another flatbed."

Abbie narrowed her eyes against the sting of wind and snow flying through the opened door. "The Hurleys? When did he leave?"

"Just before this here snow started," Mingus said. "I hauled what feed I could out to the near range in the pickup, but it's too bad to keep at it. Too bad and too dark. I hope your pa's got better sense than to try to come home in this."

Abbie nodded, worry creasing her brow. If Mingus said the storm was bad, it was bad indeed, for snow was his element. She prayed her father had made it safely to the Hurleys'. And like Mingus, she fervently hoped he wouldn't try to drive back.

"Damn," Mingus said, shaking his head, "I hope this ain't as bad as that one we had ten years back. It *feels* as bad. We'll lose some cows, I tell you, if this keeps up."

"You'd better go home and get warm," Abbie told him with concern. "You look frozen through."

Mingus left, and she shut the door, shivering from the cold. When she turned, Yates was standing in the doorway to the kitchen.

Suddenly her cheeks burned for no reason at all. She gave him a look that was half defiant, half guarded. "You startled me," she accused.

He straightened his tie. He was his old self again. He looked so crisp and neat and civilized that it was hard to imagine that he'd harnessed a horse or chopped a tree or worked beside her, mucking out stalls. It was hard to imagine him in jeans and cowboy boots at all.

He said nothing. He simply looked at her.

She turned and walked to the counter to pour herself a cup of coffee. "That was Mingus," she said, not letting herself glance at Yates. "My father went to the neighbors to borrow a flatbed."

"When?"

His voice was quiet, businesslike. She wondered why it made her feel as if someone had brushed her naked back with a feather, tickling her spine.

She set the coffeepot aside and stared down into her cup. "Just before the storm hit."

Outside, the wind howled.

''He'll be all right,'' Yates said. ''He's no fool. He's lived with this weather all his life. He won't take chances.''

She kept gazing at the cup, realizing she didn't want coffee. She wondered why she had even poured it. Nerves, that was why, pure nerves—and emotions run ragged.

''I know he won't take chances,'' she said. ''It's just...well, I never worried about him before, you know? It was Grandpa I worried about. I thought my father was so strong, so tough, he'd go on forever. It never occurred to me that he could tire out, wear out. I never thought...''

Her voice trailed off. She was almost ashamed to finish the sentence.

Yates stepped to her side at the counter. He refilled his mug with the last of the coffee. ''Yeah,'' he said gruffly. ''I thought the same thing about my father. That he was immortal. I never noticed he was getting older. Or tireder.''

She glanced up at him gratefully and was astonished to see that his expression was troubled, as if he was unhappy at what he had said.

He lifted his hand, as if he would set it on her shoulder to comfort her. But he seemed to think better of it. He shifted it away from her almost awkwardly and picked up his coffee, instead.

Abbie was relieved, yet strangely disappointed. She needed a friendly word, a friendly touch. But, when they touched, friendliness did not seem to be what they felt, and that was wrong—because of Lucky.

At that moment, the phone rang. ''Get it,'' Yates said almost harshly. ''It's probably your father.''

She gave him a brief shaky smile, then raced to the phone. She reached it by the third ring.

''Abbie?''

She felt weak with relief at hearing her father's voice. "Daddy? Are you at the Hurleys'? Are you all right?"

"Well, I'm cold as hell, but other than that . . . Mingus got back all right? Did he settle in for the night?"

"Yes."

"Good. Now look, Abbie, I'm not going to try to come home. It's too evil out there."

"I was worried about you. So was Mingus. Stay where you are until the weather breaks."

"Can you hold the fort without me?"

"Of course," she said, trying not to think that she would be alone with Yates. "Don't worry about a thing. Just take it easy. Oh, John called. He and Sandy aren't coming home for Christmas. Sandy's pregnant. She's not supposed to travel."

"Well" Frazier said, revealing no emotion. "That's news."

"And Daddy . . ."

"Yes?"

"I—I'm sorry I got angry this morning. I didn't mean to snap. I guess I've snapped a lot lately. I've been thinking more about myself than you. I really am sorry. And I *have* been worried about you. Let's not fight about Lucky or anything else. Let's just have a good Christmas."

Her father did not answer for almost half a minute. "Well," he said at last. "No reason to worry about me. None. Now, is that Connley there? I want to talk to him."

Abbie, having pushed to this frontier of frankness with her father, decided to push farther. "In a minute. Daddy, I want to ask you something. I used to think of it once in a while. Today I wondered about it a lot."

"Yes?" Frazier said, sounding apprehensive.

Abbie took a deep breath. "You've worked all your life on this ranch. It's not going to bother you to leave it behind? To live a different way?"

More silence answered her. Then Frazier gave a short, humorless laugh. "It'll be like quitting banging my head against a wall. It'll feel right good to stop."

Her heart contracted at his words, but she pressed on. "Daddy—this is what I really want to know—did you ever like it? Ever? Did you do it just because of Grandpa, or what?"

Frazier muttered something about *that* being one helluva question. "I need to talk to Connley," he said.

"No," Abbie insisted, "first tell me—I need to know. Have you spent your whole life doing something you disliked? For other people's sake?"

"Abbie, don't ask questions like that."

"I *have* to. I have to understand what you think. Please tell me."

She thought he swore, but the sound was muffled. Finally he said, "There were things I *might* have done different. I should have stayed in college. But I chose the ranch, instead. It made your grandpa happy. It made your mother happy."

"But," Abbie pleaded, "did it make *you* happy?"

Her father's voice seemed to become part bluster, part grumble. "Oh, hell, yes—for a while, I guess. But then your mother was gone, and it was...different."

"How?"

"Abbie, this is woman talk. I don't like it. Give me Connley."

"Well, I'm a woman and *I* like it," she answered. "How was it different when she was gone?"

"Hell, I don't know—it was different, is all. The *fun* went out of it. Now stop. This isn't a quiz show. Give me Connley. And behave yourself, you hear me?"

"I hear."

"Not that you'd throw over that worthless cowboy for a *real* man, a man's man. Not you."

"We promised not to argue over Lucky," she said. His remark about Yates disturbed and puzzled her. Why would her father think a bespectacled coin appraiser was more of a man than a bull rider?

Frazier's mutter was grumpy. "I'd send you to Mingus's, but the old coot lives like . . . Well, hygiene isn't on his list of priorities."

Abbie smiled in spite of herself. The biggest fight—indeed perhaps the only fight—that her father and Mingus had ever waged had not been over ranching. It had been because Mingus had let cockroaches infest his kitchen.

"I wouldn't send an animal to live there," her father grumbled. "Except maybe that miserable colt. Probably enough germs over there to kill him outright. Put Connley on."

Abbie turned, her emotions too complicated to sort out. Yates stood at the counter, putting another pot of coffee on to brew. She called to him. "My father wants to talk to you."

Yates came to the phone, and Abbie went back to the kitchen to rummage through the freezer for something for supper. She couldn't help eavesdropping. She knew her father, and she knew he was warning Yates to leave her alone. Yates, being a gentleman, would certainly promise to do so, and being a gentleman, he would keep his promise.

She heard Yates say, "Yessir," to her father. He said it a good many times.

She should have felt safe when he hung up the phone. He looked both amused and chagrined at whatever Frazier had said.

But when he looked at her over the rims of his glasses, his dark eyes catching hers, she didn't feel safe in the least.

I don't understand what's happening here, she thought with a touch of panic. *Why does he make me feel this way?*

But she willed the panic away. The only thing that existed between her and this man was an odd and prickly friendship, nothing more.

Anything else was impossible.

HE DIDN'T WANT HER to look on him as a man, dammit. He was supposed to be a neuter in her life, a sexual zero, a nonthreatening cipher. And she was supposed to be the same to him.

So he did his Mr. Perfect act, did it until he made himself sick. He did it until she, although somewhat puzzled, seemed to accept him as a creature almost without gender. It was less dangerous that way, he knew.

But no sooner had he succeeded at that, then she slipped over some line and began talking to him almost as if he were a *female* friend, for God's sake. She talked more about emotions than any woman he'd ever met, and she seemed so sincere it made him nervous, resentful. He was a studiedly unemotional man, and somehow she was penetrating his defenses.

I don't want to talk like this, he thought edgily. *I don't want to chat and be sensitive and exchange feelings. I want to kiss her until we melt all the snow in Nebraska, and maybe Colorado, too.*

But he couldn't think that, because he wasn't supposed to see her as a woman. She was part of a case, that was all.

And besides, he'd sworn to her father that he'd watch out for her; he shouldn't be lusting after her.

They had finished supper, and she'd made cherry cobbler for dessert. She was a good cook, an excellent cook, and that put him even more on edge.

She sat across from him toying with her dessert and talking about her father. "When he started hinting around, a couple of years ago, that someday he'd sell the ranch, I didn't believe him. But he kept saying it—not in front of Grandpa, of course. He said he'd keep it as long as Grandpa was alive."

Yates supposed her concern over the ranch had made her ripe for Gibbs and his fast talk. He tried to keep the moodiness out of his voice. "Was that about the time you met your... fiancé?"

Abbie brightened a bit. "Lucky? Yes." Then she grew more solemn. "But you never talk about *your* private life. Don't you have, well, somebody special?"

"No. I don't."

She gave him an odd look, and he wished he hadn't tripped out the words so brusquely. He tried to sound more casual, friendly. "So when your grandfather died, your father said he'd sell. And this time he meant it."

She shook her head pensively. "At first I couldn't believe it. But a big corporation, Agri-Comm, is going to be buying up ranches around here. And I guess he has to sell while he can."

Yates nodded.

"I was too torn up over Grandpa to really think about how my father felt all these years," she said. "I guess maybe it didn't hit me until today. When I saw him wet and tired with his hands bleeding, and then when John called..."

Yates nodded again and wished he could loosen his tie.

"But it's *hard* to understand him," Abbie said. "He doesn't like to talk about his feelings. The boys are like that, too. Lucky's not. He talks about his feelings a lot. He's easy to talk to. So are you."

Yates hated Lucky, he hated himself, he hated life. Nevertheless, he smiled, then hated his smile.

"You're kind of mysterious, though," she said.

The remark caught him off guard. The last thing he wanted to seem was mysterious. He smiled again. "Me?" he said mildly.

"You listen more than you talk. There are things I don't understand about you. For instance," she said, "you look sort of, well, Italian. But your name isn't. It's...a strange combination."

He supposed he needed to explain, to keep her satisfied. "My mother was Italian. My father was part Italian, mostly Irish."

She poured him another cup of coffee. "And you said you lost your mother? And lived with your grandparents? That must have been very hard on you."

He never spoke of the things she asked about. He didn't even know why. Now, when he had to talk, he tried to seem philosophical. "My mother was never well. At least, I can't remember when she wasn't sick. By the time I was nine, I was taking care of her more than she was of me."

"Oh," she said. "I'm sorry."

He gave a careless shrug. "Don't be. When she died, I got sent to my grandparents. I was better off there."

"But your father," she said, "why did he send you away?" She made a helpless gesture. "Or am I asking too many questions? It's just I don't know anything about you. I don't mean to pry. Or be insulting."

He set down his fork. His let his gaze meet hers. She looked so earnest, so sympathetic, that his facial muscles tensed. He felt one twitch in his cheek. "I'm not insulted. I'm flattered."

The odd thing was that in a crazy way he *did* feel flattered. He didn't understand why. He'd made a practice of never discussing the past, but he realized that he didn't exactly mind telling her. He didn't understand that, either. Maybe it was because the past was one thing he could be honest about.

Still, he was surprised at how hard the words came to him. "My father couldn't keep me. He was a police officer. He kept crazy hours. Stakeouts, stuff like that. A housekeeper would have raised me. Hell, a housekeeper had already done most of the raising. I guess he thought enough was enough."

"But you must have missed him and your mother terribly."

For the first time, he felt true emotion register on his face. He willed it away, forcing his expression to be calm, neutral. "I can't remember her that well. She was so...fragile. She got sick about a year after I was born. When my father was gone, the house always seemed...the house was... Well, was—it wasn't home."

"Oh, Yates," Abbie breathed, "I'm sorry."

He kept his expression normal. He waved her concern away, picked up his fork and stirred the last crumbs of cobbler. "No. He did the right thing. My grandparents were good people. I had a good time. I stayed with them until my father remarried. My stepmother's a decent woman. She ran a stamp-and-coin shop. I worked for her after school. It's not like I was deprived."

She seemed more sympathetic than before. Lord, did she look at Lucky Gibbs like that? The little weasel was crazy to lie to her, use her. Didn't the fool see what he had?

"I don't see how you can be so calm about it," she said, admiration in her voice. "Daddy and the boys and I haven't always peacefully coexisted, but I can't imagine life without them all. Your father—you get along with him?"

He shrugged. "Yeah." Once again he found his words coming with difficulty. "I guess I—what?—hero-worshipped him. My grandparents idolized him. He was their only child."

"He was? You mean he's . . . passed on?"

He frowned at the euphemism; it was against his nature to mince words. "He's dead. Eight years. Just about the time I finished college. My stepmother remarried. She lives in Bermuda."

"Your grandparents—on the ranch," she said, as if trying to put the pieces together. "Are they—still alive?"

"My grandmother died a few months after my father. I think—" he fought against gritting his teeth, for he had never said these words aloud before "—maybe the loss killed her."

"And your grandfather?"

"He died. Two and a half years ago."

"You're *all* alone?"

"I don't mind." That, at least, was true. He'd been a loner since he was a child. He'd grown quite accomplished at being a loner.

"And the ranch?"

He couldn't repress a bitter laugh. "He left it to me. I finally sold it. Thought the damn thing would never sell."

"You sold it? Didn't you feel as if you were selling a part of yourself?"

He shrugged. He hadn't felt anything about selling the land. He hadn't allowed himself to. "What's past is past."

His words seemed to sadden her. "What's past is past," she repeated. "Well, at least, we've got one Christmas left here. I hope, afterward, we'll keep some of the traditions. We used to have what Grandpa called the Three Great Tasks at Christmas. One was getting the tree. He and I and John did that. The next one my brother Preston and I do. That's decorating the house and barn—"

Yates frowned. "The barn?"

She smiled. "It's something my mother started, years ago. A wreath for every stall. After all, she said, Christmas began in a stable."

He smiled back, almost unwillingly. "And the third Great Task?"

She looked happier, remembering. "Wrapping the presents. We're *great* present wrappers. It's like a contest—who can do it fanciest. I mean, we have to have the paper on them, first, so nobody knows what's inside, but the ribbons and bows and decorations—you wouldn't believe them."

She looked so pleased at the thought of Christmas that he wanted to wince. He should be long gone by Christmas; it was a full week away. By Christmas, she would know the truth about Lucky Gibbs. She wouldn't be smiling then.

She'd know the truth about Yates, too. He pushed that thought from his mind. He kept his expression bland, false. "If it's a contest, who usually wins?" he asked.

"My brother Adon," she said ruefully. "Every year. Nobody can top him. One year he—"

The phone rang again. Yates gritted his teeth and hoped it wasn't Lucky Gibbs.

When he'd started this charade, all he'd wanted was enough evidence to convict the slimeball. Now he'd like to land a couple of punches that would rearrange Gibbs's pretty, lying face.

"Excuse me." Abbie rose eagerly, setting her napkin beside the plate. Yates felt an intense surge of relief when she left the room. He did not watch her go.

Instead, he stared broodingly around the kitchen. A homey place, he had to admit.

He remembered his grandmother's kitchen. At Christmastime, it was filled with tantalizing smells. His grandmother had loved him so extravagantly he'd been embarrassed. He never knew how to return so much affection, so he pretended he felt little.

He hadn't even let her kiss him goodbye when he left to live with his father and stepmother. He'd been too old—seventeen. He hadn't told his grandparents he'd miss them. He'd been too tough to say things like that. Ever since he could remember, he'd been too tough to feel at all, if he could help it.

So what? he asked himself contemptuously. It was the smart way to be, wasn't it? Why was he kicking himself because he was going to hurt some blue-eyed country girl? It was her own fault for being stupid enough to fall for Lucky Gibbs.

As for himself, it wasn't sympathy he was feeling; it was lust. Lust in disguise, he told himself. She didn't stir his heart—she stirred his sex drive. He needed to keep his cynicism intact.

But from the next room, he could hear her talking, and although he couldn't make out the words, he detected unhappiness in her voice. He turned up his hearing aid, but still couldn't catch what she said.

Instinctively, he rose and went to her. He stood at her side, looking down at her.

"Of course, I understand," she said with strained cheer. Tears glinted in her eyes. "Merry Christmas, anyway. Sure. Of course. I love you."

Whoever was on the phone answered by saying something that made her raise her chin. "I *know* we don't say things like that in this family. That's why I said it. I meant it. 'Bye, Preston. Give Marcie my best and tell her I'm sorry."

She set the receiver back in its cradle. She didn't meet Yates's eyes. He could tell she was fighting back tears. It gave him an unpleasant knot in his throat.

"What's wrong?" he asked.

"My brother Preston. They can't come home for Christmas. His wife's mother has to have surgery. They're going there, instead."

Yates looked at her mouth, set in a line determined not to tremble. "They don't have much choice," he said quietly.

She nodded. "I know. They're doing what's right. Her place is with her family. And Preston's place is with her."

"But you'll miss him."

"I'll miss him. We've never had a Christmas without him. Well, we'll make up for it another year."

"Sure."

"It's just that it's the last Christmas in this house..."

"I know."

"And the first one without Grandpa. Or John. And now Preston." Her voice shook slightly when she said Preston's name.

"I know."

He couldn't help himself. He knew he was going to take her into his arms. His heart hammered so hard it seemed to close off his throat. He couldn't breathe, his blood roared in his ears, and he felt empty with need.

He put one hand on her upper arm and drew her to him, almost against his will. He wound his other arm around her waist, pulling her close. Yet his embrace was careful, almost hesitant, as if he feared she'd break away.

Instead, she put her arms on his shoulders and pressed her face against his chest. Something seemed to die in him, he wanted her so badly. Slowly, he began to bend to capture her lips. Devil take the consequences, he thought. He couldn't stop himself. He just couldn't.

But her words did.

"If only Lucky could be here," she said, her voice breaking. "Oh, I'm sorry. I just can't help it."

His heart turned to ice. He raised his head and stared unseeingly at the decorated tree. He kept himself from pulling her nearer. He went as motionless as if carved of stone.

He held her in his arms while she cried for another man. The man he had come to destroy. For the sake of justice.

And vengeance.

CHAPTER SEVEN

ABBIE DIDN'T CRY, although she wanted to. She pressed her face against Yates's snowy shirtfront, gripped his shoulders tightly and squeezed her eyes shut, trying to marshal her self-control.

It was Lucky's arms she should be in, not Yates's. But Lucky was thousands of miles away. Yates, in his stiff-mannered way, was the one who had offered consolation, and she had accepted it without question.

She clung to him for a long moment, saying nothing. He held her, his muscles taut, his embrace formal, almost awkward, as if touching her was unpleasant. He held himself so rigidly she quickly sensed his unease.

And yet she could not bring herself to break away from him immediately. His embrace was not a cuddly one, like Lucky's, and he did not mumble nonsensical sweet nothings in her ear as Lucky always did.

Yet in spite of how rigidly he held her, there was something oddly comforting in his touch. He was far too tall; being next to him shouldn't have felt right, but it did. She discerned great strength in his body, but it was of a different sort than Lucky's, deeper, more dependable . . .

She broke away from him then, ashamed of her thoughts, her feelings. Comparing Yates with Lucky was disloyal to Lucky. And going into another man's arms seemed downright unfaithful, a weakness in herself she should despise and not tolerate.

"Sorry," she said unhappily, not looking at him.

"It's all right." He sounded as ill at ease as she felt.

"Well," she said with a toss of her head, "it's too bad. But Adon's still coming. And Laurel. And their two boys. The kids are always fun. I mean, Christmas is really for children, right?"

"I suppose."

"And we'll have the gift wrapping. That's always the funnest part. Almost more fun than opening things. Maybe it really is better to give than to receive."

"So they say."

She turned toward the kitchen. He stepped in front of the door, blocking her path. His eyes, behind the glasses, were serious, concerned. "What are you going to do?"

She shrugged. "Clean up the dishes. Feed the colt. Then get out the decorations. If Preston's not here, I'll do the decorating myself."

"Abbie, it's almost nine o'clock. I'll help you with the colt. Then you should rest."

"I don't want to rest. I don't feel like resting. I want to do something, anything."

Once again he seemed about to reach for her, then stopped himself. "Abbie, listen. Last night you passed out. Don't keep pushing yourself."

"I'm fine," she said more curtly than she should have and shouldered her way past him. "And please don't help me with the horse. I'd like some time to myself."

Why did he have to be so blasted *considerate?* And when he was, why did it throw her into such turmoil?

She busied herself with the dishes. When she came out, she saw the office light on. Yates was a great one to talk, she thought irritably; he never stopped working, either.

He respected her wishes. He let her feed the colt alone. Then she went outside to feed Oogly, the shy black dog that lived under the porch. She came back in and warmed up, and still he stayed in the office. But when she went to the hall and lowered the ladder that led to the attic, she found him at her side again.

"What?" she said ungraciously. She cast him a suspicious glance. His clothes were still immaculate, but his beard was starting to shadow his jaw. He had a heavy beard compared to Lucky. She found herself imagining how it would scratch and tickle if his face were next to hers.

What a stupid thing to think, she told herself angrily. She turned away from him and started up the ladder.

"I suppose you're going to lug stuff down that ladder," he said, sarcasm in his tone.

"I suppose I am," she said without looking back.

"You know, your father asked me to watch out for you."

"I don't need watching out for," she said, reaching the attic. But the boxes, packed and neatly stacked, were bigger than she recalled. Preston, not she, had always carried them downstairs.

Last year, she remembered, with a pang of guilt, she had wanted Lucky to help her and Preston and Marcie, but he'd refused. He said he'd hurt his back the week before in Houston. They'd worked, and he'd sat in the office talking to her grandfather.

Preston had made barbed remarks. He said that every time Lucky was around when work was to be done, he conveniently had a bad back, a bad shoulder or something else to keep him on the sidelines.

Drat, she scolded herself. Another thought that seemed less than loyal. Lucky couldn't help it. He was in a dangerous profession; he frequently got hurt. Besides, his visits to SkyRim were the only time he ever had to relax, and her grandfather had enjoyed his company.

She grimaced and tried to push a stack of boxes closer to the attic's open trapdoor. The attic was dusty, and she sneezed as she strained to move them.

Uninvited, Yates came into the attic. He ducked his head to dodge the low beams and effortlessly transferred the boxes next to the open door.

"Don't," Abbie protested. "You'll get all dusty."

"And you'll fall down the ladder and break your neck," he muttered. "I'll take these."

"You don't have to—"

"Don't argue." He spoke with such finality that she held her peace.

One by one he wrestled the boxes down the ladder. She saw that she could never have managed without him. He got dust on his dark slacks and dirt smudges on his white shirt. He even had a cobweb in his dark curls, and she had to resist the impulse to wipe it away.

He'd been so kind to help her with the boxes, though, she couldn't refuse his help in putting up the decorations, although she tried.

"It's late," she said.

"I'm not tired."

"Then go work with that computer."

"I'm sick of that bloody computer," he said with surprising passion.

"All right." Abbie sighed. "First we've got these holly garlands to hang. They go around the top of the wall. There are little nails up there to hold them."

She opened the garland box. There were countless yards of garlands with dark green leaves and bright red berries.

Yates whistled softly. "Where'd you get this? You've got enough to drape half the state."

Abbie smiled in spite of herself. "My mother. There used to be a department store in Bison City. When it went out of business, it sold everything, even its Christmas decorations. Mama came home with half of them—she was so excited."

Yates lowered a brow sardonically. "She bought *half* the decorations in the store?"

"Well, a good part of them. We even used to have a life-size Rudolph the Red-Nosed Reindeer. But my nephews broke his head off accidentally."

Abbie and Yates had to stand on chairs to hang the holly. He kept admonishing her to be careful. She kept telling him not to worry so much. He insisted on doing the places that were hardest to reach. Resigned, she let him.

But they soon fell into a comfortable rhythm, and she could not help feeling companionable toward him. They broke at eleven o'clock to care for Frosty, and this time she let Yates help. He was so efficient things seemed twice as easy with his help.

They put wreaths and lights at the windows and set up the little manger scene. Her mother had collected the figurines when she herself was a child. They were old and the worse for wear, but Abbie loved them and would not have traded them for ones of silver or gold.

"See this shepherd—how he's kind of chewed up?" Abbie said, showing the small object to Yates. "My brother John used it for a teething toy when he was little. And this angel? Preston had a border collie. When it was a pup, it chewed her wings off. I guess she has to be an earth angel now."

"An earth angel," Yates said, looking first at it, then at her.

Something in his eyes confused her and made her strangely nervous. She looked away. "And this camel—we had to glue his hind legs back on. John hit Adon on the head with him.''

''Hardly the Christmas spirit.''

''Daddy said the Christmas story had three wise men, but with my brothers he was stuck with three wise guys.''

''And an earth angel?''

The compliment took her aback. Her mouth twitched in a self-conscious smile. ''He never called me an angel. Usually the opposite. I could be just as rough-and-tumble as the boys.''

''I bet you could.'' He smiled.

His smile made her heart do a cartwheel. She looked away and shook her head. ''Look. Setting this up doesn't really take any effort. Why don't you go to bed?''

''I'm not sleepy.''

''Then take another try at that computer. You don't have to help me anymore.''

''I told you, I hate the rotten computer. Besides, there's still a whole box of wreaths.''

''Those are for the barn. We can't do that tonight.''

For a moment, neither of them said anything. They listened to the wind's incessant keening around the house.

Abbie put the figures of Joseph and Mary in place and rearranged a pair of sheep. She could feel Yates watching her.

She licked her lips. ''Could I ask you something?''

''I suppose.''

''You say you hate that computer. It's like you don't really *like* your job that much. Why do you do it?''

He took so long to answer she wondered if she'd offended him. She glanced up and saw his expression was inexplicably troubled.

''Let's just say that this is what I have to do—for now,'' he said at last.

"For now? You mean you're going to do something else?"

Again he paused before he spoke. "As a matter of fact, I am."

She set the last of the lambs in place. "What?" she asked, wondering why he seemed so reluctant to talk.

He shrugged and made a gesture that seemed to say, *it's not important.* "I'm going to buy into a security company."

She looked at him with fresh curiosity. "Security—you mean, like stocks and bonds?"

He shook his head, and still seemed uncomfortable talking about it. "No. Security as in electronic guard systems. House and business. Alarms."

She cocked her head, puzzled. "Guard systems? Isn't that a big leap from coins? How did you ever decide to do that?"

"I've got . . . something of an interest in it, that's all."

"Do you think you'll like it?"

"I don't know. It seems like a good investment. It'll give me more freedom."

"To do what?"

"I don't know yet. Maybe I'll take up golf. Or jogging. I don't know."

"But I don't understand," she said, smiling at her own lack of comprehension. "From coins to burglar alarms. What connection is there?"

He fell into silence. When he looked at her again, his face was serious, almost grim. "Listen," he said, then paused as if searching for the right words.

He took a deep breath. "Let me tell you a story. Dealing coins—it's a strange business."

"I suppose it is. I never thought about it."

"The market for coins goes up and down. It's cyclical. Right now, we're in a downswing. Prices are low."

"Business is bad? That's why you're getting out?"

"Not exactly. In the last decade, prices were good. Dealers could make money. But then things changed. Too many dealers, not enough customers."

"Yes?" She wondered why he seemed so solemn and chose his words so carefully.

He frowned, staring at the Christmas scene. "A couple of years ago, a series of break-ins occurred. A lot of coin stores got hit, robbed. All over the country."

"Yes?"

"But they weren't really robbed. It was a scam. For insurance money. Instead of going bankrupt, these people were getting fat insurance claims and walking away with a big bundle of cash."

"They were robbing themselves?"

"No. They hired somebody. He made a business of it. A man named Claridge was a dealer in Omaha. Do you remember that name?"

Abbie, too, frowned. "Vaguely...yes."

"Claridge and his partner, Robbins, *arranged* these break-ins. Robbins did the actual burglaries. They got a nice chunk of the insurance money—and kept whatever got stolen. They had two businesses on the side—burglary and running a profitable black market in rare merchandise."

"They sold the coins?"

"Secretly. Some of this stuff was rare. Worth tens of thousands of dollars. It couldn't go back on the open market—experts would notice. Plus, it had been reported stolen. But Claridge could approach somebody privately and say he had a source, and the source was willing to sell for an attractive price."

"Did people *know* they were buying stolen property?"

He gave a cynical shrug. "Some did. They didn't care. Claridge had sweet merchandise at sweet prices."

"I think I remember," Abbie said, touching an angel with a fingertip. "Wasn't the FBI involved?"

"First the insurance companies, then the FBI. Claridge couldn't keep his operation hidden forever. For one thing, there's a big computer network out there on coins. When stolen things start turning up, people notice. The word gets out."

Abbie picked up the angel, running her fingertips over its faded paint. She did it out of nervousness. She didn't know why Yates's story made her uneasy, or why he was so intense as he told it.

The news story was coming back to her in bits and pieces, and she recalled hazily that it had bizarre aspects. "Wasn't there something strange about Claridge? And didn't he have some sort of complicated system for getting all this done?" she asked.

"Right," Yates said. "Claridge was a big man, a huge man. He weighed almost three hundred pounds. After about two years of burglaries, he and Robbins had a car accident. Pure fluke. Robbins died. Claridge lost a leg. A one-legged guy that size doesn't slip around easily. Or unnoticed. The burglaries stopped. But he kept on selling stolen goods—and started receiving more from other sources."

"And he had accomplices?"

Yates nodded. "The newspapers called it the Stewardess Caper. He had two stewardesses working for him— carrying stolen coins, bringing the cash back to him. Always cash—he didn't want to leave a trail."

"That's right. The stewardesses. And the Claridge man got shot. And so did an FBI man, and another got hurt, didn't he?"

Yates's mouth took on a bitter twist. "Yeah. One dead. Claridge shot him. Another—an undercover Nebraska policeman—was hurt. And Claridge was killed. Nobody'd expected him to put up a fight. They thought it would be a routine bust. It wasn't."

Abbie studied the angel. "I remember. He said something dramatic, like he'd rather die than live in jail. And there was another man with him. He got away."

"Yeah. Another man. He got away."

"I remember seeing the pictures of the stewardesses. I felt sorry for them. They were young. And pretty. It's a shame—they ruined their lives."

"They were his couriers. They were perfect for it—could travel from city to city, and nobody thought anything of it. But there was a third courier, one authorities never found. A man. He could be mean, dangerous. He beat one customer half to death for trying to underpay. The authorities nicknamed him the Enforcer. Claridge used him when things looked like they might get rough. He was there the night they took Claridge. He did some of the shooting."

Abbie set the angel before the manger. She wondered why he narrated the story with such a strange combination of reluctance and passion. "How could he get away like that?"

"The only officer that saw him died. Claridge shot him. The Enforcer hit another officer from behind and got away. It was chaos. There were two officers down. And Claridge."

"But that's terrible. The customer who was beaten— couldn't *he* describe him?"

Yates shook his head. "He wouldn't. Guy scared him. Scared him badly."

"Wouldn't the stewardesses tell?"

"They knew he existed, that was all. They didn't know his name."

Abbie knelt and started to check the boxes to make sure she hadn't missed anything. "Well, I certainly hope they catch him," she said, rustling through the paper.

Yates was silent a moment. "They will," he said. "They will."

"But what's this have to do with you? Did someone try to pass stolen things on to you?"

His eyes met hers. He fingered his hearing aid. "No. That's not it."

A small frisson trembled through her. It was almost as if he was asking her to decipher some secret message in the story. But what? What connection did he want her to make?

Suddenly a terrible thought swept through her mind. She looked at him with horror. "Oh, no. No. You don't think *Grandpa* traded for something stolen—do you? I mean if he did it was purely by accident. He was always extremely honest—"

"No, Abbie, no. And I believe you. I'm not accusing him of anything. Still, it's possible he could have gotten something accidentally. If anything does show up in the inventory, it would have to be returned."

Relief coursed through her. "Of course. I'd want it that way. It'd be the only honest thing to do."

"Honest," he repeated, his tone mocking. But he didn't look mocking. His expression was stony, almost forbidding.

"I mean, if you told me that story so I wouldn't be shocked if something *did* turn up—"

He cut her off, shaking his head. "That's not why I told you. I told you because, well, so that you can see that coins and security systems aren't so unrelated. If those stores had had proper security, Claridge could never have pulled the robberies off. The insurance companies require security systems now. It's good business."

He rose and went to the door of the sun porch, staring out moodily. Abbie watched him, uncertain what to think. She supposed his explanation made sense. Yet she sensed that the conversation had carried more emotional freight than he admitted. She didn't understand how or why.

"That's . . . that's the only reason you told me all this?" she asked warily. "To make that point? About security systems?"

He kept his back to her. "That's the reason."

"Oh."

He kept staring at the frost-covered windows. "You should get some sleep, Abbie. In a bed. I'll give the colt his next feeding."

She, too, stood. "No. You should sleep yourself."

He shook his head. "No. I'll work on the computer some more."

"But you said—"

"I've got my second wind. I feel like going at it again."

"And if you can't get into the disc?"

He lifted one shoulder in a gesture of resignation. "Then I'll go through the collection cold, and hope you've got a good memory. I don't want it to come to that."

"I don't, either," she said. Her heart beat unaccountably hard. "Thank you for helping me."

But he, who was usually so polite, said nothing in return. He kept his back to her. Abbie's chest tightened in confusion.

"Good night," she said at last.

He nodded, but didn't speak.

She had to pass him to get to her temporary bed on the sun porch. When she did, she kept her head down, so she wouldn't have to look at him.

She was surprised and almost frightened when his hand shot out and captured her arm, just above the wrist.

"What?" she asked, looking at him in alarm.

He bent closer to her, his dark eyes intent. "Abbie, I... What would happen if Lucky was out of the picture? What if, say, he found somebody else?"

His touch made her pulses leap so wildly she shook.

"That would never happen," she said raggedly. "I love him, and he loves me."

"Things don't always turn out the way we expect," he said from between his teeth.

"This will. I love him. He loves me."

He bent toward her. "All right. But it's a hypothetical question. What if...?"

"There is no if," she retorted, wondering why her voice sounded so desperate. "I love him. And he loves me. That's the bottom line."

His hand tightened around her wrist. "Abbie...if... if..." He bent nearer still. "My God," he said raggedly, "the world is nothing except ifs..." He didn't finish what he'd started to say. He didn't because he was about to kiss her.

A world full of ifs is a world full of danger, Abbie thought, yet she could not turn from him. Instead, almost against her will, she found herself lifting her face to him.

His mouth captured hers with such sweet ferocity that she had to close her eyes to keep from becoming dizzy. His lips were warm, intoxicating, magically ravishing.

No, no, no, she thought. Yet she also thought, *Yes, yes. Oh, yes.*

Ordinary reality fell away. The blizzard still howled around the house, but she no longer heard it. Cold seeping through the porch windows had cast a chill on the living room, but she no longer felt it.

The outside world was windswept and deathly white with snow, but she was transported. His kiss took her to a place that, instead, was warm and dark and velvety.

His hand tightened on her waist as his kiss deepened, drawing her more completely into the spell his touch had cast.

His mouth against hers was both impetuous and tender; it was provocative yet gentle. It promised danger; it promised safety. It demanded everything of her; it demanded nothing.

His arms wound around her, pulling her against his long body. Her breasts pressed against his chest, and her hands tightened involuntarily on his biceps. The starchy fabric of his shirt was crisp beneath her fingers, and his muscles taut with power.

Abbie's very heart trembled. *Honey and fire,* she thought in confusion. *Kissing him is like honey and fire.*

She rose on her tiptoes so his fervent lips could burn her more sweetly, more hotly. The motion, slight as it was, seemed to inflame him, and for an instant, his touch communicated a desire so intense it shook her soul.

Then he drew his mouth from hers and pressed his cheek against her hair. He held her, simply held her, and she rested, eyes shut, against his chest.

The pose was peaceful, but Abbie's mind was filled with dark tumult. Yates, too, was troubled; she could sense it. She kept her eyes firmly shut and clung to him as tightly as he did to her.

She felt as if she were on the edge of some precarious abyss. As long as she didn't move, as long as she didn't think about what she was doing, she was not completely lost.

The phone rang. Abbie started guiltily from Yates's arms and he let her go. His hands fell to his sides, his fists clenched. His glasses were crooked, but somehow they gave him an air of intensity that was barely controlled.

Her face was hot, and she could not bear to look at him. Ashamed, confused, she picked up the phone.

"Hello?" Her voice sounded as if it belonged to someone else.

"Hello, honey," said Lucky. "Tell me how much you love me. I need to hear your voice, sweet angel girl."

CHAPTER EIGHT

ABBIE, STRICKEN, opened her mouth but could not speak. Her blood pounded in her ears.

"Hear me, sugar? How much do you love me?"

Abbie passed a hand over her eyes. This was Lucky, the man she loved, the man she would marry, the man she had promised never to betray.

"I—" she squeezed her eyes shut, knowing Yates stood behind her, listening to each word "—love you very much." She drew a breath, but her chest was so constricted with guilt the action hurt. "I'll love you forever."

"And then some?"

"And then some," she agreed through clenched teeth. *Oh, God,* she kept thinking, *what have I done? What have I done?*

"Just had the urge to call you, babe," he said. "I'm a little down. A little blue."

Abbie's eyes snapped open in alarm. "Down? Blue? What's wrong?" A hoard of possible disasters stampeded through her imagination.

"Well, hon," he said ruefully, "I had a little accident. Gonna stay here longer than I thought."

"Accident?" She was horrified.

"Hell," Lucky said, his tone turning resentful. "Tried to ride a surfboard. Figured if I can ride a bull, a surfboard's a cinch, right? Let me tell you, those waves can *buck.*"

This is punishment for what I've done, Abbie thought in remorse. *It's my fault he's hurt.*

"What happened? How bad is it?" she asked.

"I got tossed off and the dang thing came down at me. Was gonna hit me smack in the face—"

"Oh," Abbie gasped. Lucky had a face of such beauty she could not stand to think of it marred. And he had a healthy vanity about it, as well he should.

"So I put up my arm," Lucky said, "but it still hit me. In the eye. Detached a retina, the doctor says."

"Oh, Lucky," Abbie almost wailed. He couldn't ride with a detached retina. It was impossible; he could permanently injure his eye. It would be weeks before he could go on the rodeo circuit again.

Tears stung her eyes. She kept her back to Yates, feeling more miserable with each passing moment. "Are you in the hospital?" she asked, her voice choked.

"Yeah. For observation. They're going let me go tomorrow."

"Then you'll come home?"

If he came back, everything would return to normal, she thought desperately.

"What good would that do?" he asked. "I can't ride. I can't make any money. The Fettermans want me to stay with them. I might as well."

"The Fettermans?"

"Yeah. The rancher. The rich guy. I was playing around with his kids when this happened. They kind of blame themselves. Besides, what choice have I got? This is the guy who buys my return ticket, right?"

"Oh," Abbie said, sick with disappointment. "But for how long? Couldn't you buy a ticket back yourself? I mean, I could take care of you."

"Abbie, *why?*" Lucky's tone was impatient. "Spend all that money just to go to Nebraska and freeze my tail off?"

"I don't like to think of you hurt and so far away."

"Look, why spend money? I'll have free room, free meals, a free ride back. And this *is* Hawaii. Even if I'm stuck here alone in this damn hospital while everybody else parties."

"Parties?"

"One of Fetterman's kids is having a birthday party at the hotel. Big bash." He swore again. "I *hate* hospitals. I hate being hurt."

"I know." She bit her lip, remembering. He had often been restless and moody when he'd been hurt in Bison City. He'd said then that she was the only thing that kept him sane.

"I'm here in this bed," he complained, "looking out the window. It's a great night. I can see orchid trees, palm trees, moonlight. But I'm stuck here."

She tried to console him. "It's dark night here. We're having a blizzard, a bad one."

Lucky gave a bitter laugh. "At least I'm spared that. Ouch. Jeez, that hurts."

Abbie winced in sympathy. "What hurts?"

"My head. When I laugh. Nothin' fun about bein' here alone. Especially when everybody else…" He paused, not finishing the sentence.

"Especially when what?" she asked, her voice choking.

"Especially when you're so far away," he said smoothly. "This is really a bummer, honey. Reminds me of when I was a little kid. When I broke my leg. My dad was in jail, my dumb mom had to work. I just lay there, with that cast, all by myself. She'd leave me there in front of the television with a six-pack of warm root beer and a box of crackers. I lived on root beer and crackers for a month. God, I still hate layin' around.''

Abbie closed her eyes in misery. Lucky had often told her of his broken leg. It seemed to haunt him, a symbol of all his childhood neglect and unhappiness.

"I'm so sorry," she said. And she was sorry, for his past and present suffering, and for her own foolish inexcusable infidelity.

"Tell me all the sweet things I like to hear, sugar."

She shifted uncomfortably, too conscious that Yates stood behind her, listening. *Let him listen,* she thought rebelliously. *Lucky's the one I love. What happened with Yates was an accident, a stupid ugly accident. It meant nothing.*

"You're handsome," she said with all the conviction she could. She knew what he wanted to hear. He'd asked her to recite the same litany many times, whenever his fragile ego needed tenderness. "You're handsome and smart and fearless and the best rodeo rider west of the Mississippi."

"You forgot charming," he said.

"Oh, of course," she said, chagrined. "You're handsome and smart and charming and fearless and the best rodeo rider west of the Mississippi."

"That's better."

"Lucky, you're sure you're not hurt worse than you're telling me?"

"I'll be okay if I take it easy. And I plan to do just that. Oh, and, Abbie, I want a favor."

"Yes?" She wished Yates would have the decency to leave the room. His presence seemed to draw all the oxygen out of the air.

"In your grandpa's safe, I got a roll of buffalo nickels. They're labeled. They're in bad shape, not worth much— fifteen, twenty dollars, maybe. Send 'em to me by Federal

Express, will you? Fetterman's youngest daughter collects coins. I promised her some. Don't open 'em or anything—just send the roll. It's the least I can do. Send it in care of the Fetterman Ranch, I'll give you the address. Got a pencil? Write it down, sweetness.''

Abbie fumbled for a pencil and wrote down the address he gave, but her mind spun in confusion. She was surprised that Lucky had anything in her grandfather's safe; she couldn't remember his ever mentioning it before.

''Send it right away,'' he said.

''But...I...'' she stammered. ''There's a blizzard. I can't. Not yet.''

''As soon as you can, sugar. Do it for your Lucky. You do love me, don't you, sugar? Me and only me? Forever and ever?''

A pained expression tightened the corners of her mouth. ''Of course—''

He interrupted her, suddenly cheerful. ''Hey—looks like I've got a visitor. Gotta hang up. Call you sometime soon. And do what I asked, okay? A special little someone's waitin' for that surprise.''

She did not have a chance to answer. The line went dead. She hung up the receiver and squared her shoulders. She turned to face Yates, her manner cold, condescending.

''Were you happy with yourself, eavesdropping?''

His dark eyes didn't waver. ''No.'' He tapped his hearing aid. ''This works too well. I didn't much like what I heard.''

She rubbed the back of her hand across her mouth, as if wiping away his kiss. ''Then we're even. I didn't much like what you did.''

He hooked his thumbs on either side of his belt buckle. His expression was as stony as hers. ''You seemed to like it. Until lover boy called.'' He nodded at the phone, disgust in the line of his mouth.

She drew herself up taller. "What happened between you and me—"

"Meant nothing," he finished for her. "Nothing at all. We were tired, we were wired, you miss him—" he gave the phone another sardonic nod "—and for a minute things went strange on us. No harm done. Repeat—it meant nothing."

"Nothing at all."

"In the meantime, want some advice?"

"Not from you."

"Take it, anyway. You can do better."

Abbie's eyes narrowed. "I don't know what you mean."

"I mean Gibbs. You can do better than him."

She tossed her head contemptuously. "You don't even know him."

"So now he's hurt," Yates said, his upper lip curling. "And he wants sympathy. But not enough to come back here and get it in person. Staying in Hawaii, is he? While you work yourself to a frazzle, and your father—"

"Stop it!" she snapped. She pointed to her grandfather's office. "Get in there and do whatever you're paid to do. Or go to bed. But stay out of my way and out of my life, and don't eavesdrop on my private conversations. You don't even know what he said, so you—"

"I didn't have to," Yates shot back, his shoulders lifting in a militant shrug. "I could tell that as conversations go, it was one-sided. About nothing except *him*. Did he ask you one question about yourself? Even one?"

Abbie paled. With cruel accuracy he had struck her most vulnerable spot. She didn't want to think about his accusation; she refused to. It would only fill her with doubts.

"This isn't your business," she said with as much dignity as she could.

"Right," he said. "But this appraisal comes free of charge. Does he know what you're going through here? That your father's trapped by this damned blizzard? Does he care there *is* a blizzard? Does he know about the colt you're breaking your back to save? Does he know I'm here—another man—alone with you? Does he ever talk about one damned thing except himself?"

"He's hurt," Abbie retorted, clenching her fists. "He's hurt and he's all alone, thousands of miles away. He doesn't know how long he'll be laid up. He's had such a hard life—"

Yates gave a short disbelieving laugh. "Abbie, he's in *Hawaii,* for God's sake. He went there without even telling you. This guy's sitting pretty. How can a girl as smart as you—"

"He *needs* me!" she said furiously. "Nobody understands him—none of you. People have failed him his whole life long. I won't. Nobody's ever stuck by him. I will. Nobody ever considers the kind of life he's led. I do."

Yates laughed again. She could have slapped him.

She no longer knew at whom she should be most angry: herself, Yates, perhaps even Lucky. But it was easiest to strike out at Yates, and his taunts invited aggression. Why had *he* turned against Lucky so suddenly? Was it to justify his own actions? She felt a surge of something akin to hatred for him.

Yates smiled caustically. "Sympathy's a wonderful thing, Abbie. So's the need to nurture. But too much of anything is dangerous. Even—you'll pardon the expression—love."

The air between them seemed to shake with antagonism. She searched for something to say that would hurt

him as much as he'd hurt her. "Maybe you're just jealous," she said. "Because he's a real man, not a stuffed
shirt. He rides bulls. You push pencils. He takes chances.
You take inventories. Go play with your computer. I've got
more important things in my life than lists."

She stalked to the porch. Behind her, she heard Yates
swear, curtly but with passion.

YATES INTENDED to work all night. He didn't feel like
sleeping; he wanted to know what Old Mylo had officially
logged in his collection and compare it with what was really there. He had to prove that Mylo had once owned
coins like those that later turned up as stolen property in
Texas.

He would get the goods on Gibbs, and then he wanted
to get the hell out. And he wouldn't look back.

He stared at the screen and gritted his teeth. He'd been
a fool to tell the girl the story. He shouldn't have taken the
chance. He was an idiot. He was worse.

He knew why he'd done it. Part of the reason might
seem noble, but was in truth phony and self-serving. He
didn't want her taken completely by surprise when Gibbs
was arrested. He didn't want her thrown into total shock.
He had tried—in an admittedly roundabout way—to warn
her.

But then, to his own disgust, he had to make things
worse by making a pass at her. How in the name of all that
was holy had he been stupid enough to kiss her?

His more carnal self asked a harder question: *How, in
the name of all that was human, could he have stopped
himself?*

His carnal self, he thought with contempt, was a
schmuck.

All he'd wanted, initially, was to warn Abbie that Lucky Gibbs wouldn't come back to SkyRim. But in truth, he wanted her to forget Gibbs. Yates wanted her for himself.

The fact made him sick. Yet he couldn't deny it. Sometimes he'd look at her and think his blood had turned to a river of fire. He'd be carrying on a polite conversation with her, but in his mind he was making love to her until they were both half-faint from it.

And it wasn't simply that he desired her. He *liked* her. He had seldom ever desired the women he liked or liked the women he desired. Life was simpler that way.

But Abbie had ambushed him emotionally. She was beautiful and spirited, and he liked her compassion, her strength, her struggle to do the right thing.

He wasn't used to caring for another person. People who cared got hurt. The security business was exactly right for him—a career in which things were kept locked up inside.

When he'd left the ranch and his grandparents, he'd never looked back. Abbie Hale was made of different stuff than he. She was always caring, always remembering, always looking back—or forward. Perversely, he both admired her and pitied her for it.

He wished he could shield her, but it was impossible. He was crazy to involve himself with her at all.

Two men were lying to her. Lucky was one; he was the other.

He had no business wanting to take her in his arms as if he would never hurt her, never deceive her. And he was doing all these things.

ABBIE HAD FALLEN asleep clutching the alarm clock. Waking, she groped for it. When she couldn't find it, she panicked, threw back the quilt and swiftly rose.

She switched on the porch light and saw the clock on the wicker table. She was astonished; it was after six.

Impossible, she thought groggily. She rubbed her eyes and headed for the kitchen. Something must be wrong with the clock. That was the only answer.

In the kitchen doorway, she bumped into Yates. Their bodies collided with such force that she staggered backward. His left arm shot out to catch her. Still half dazed with sleep, she looked up into his face.

Frown lines were etched into his forehead, and behind his glasses, his dark eyes were shadowed. Stubble roughened his jaw. His shirtsleeves were rolled to the elbows, and he held a bottle of formula. When Abbie recovered her balance, he let go of her as swiftly as if she had scalded him. His expression was disapproving.

"What are you doing?" Abbie demanded, wiping back a loose strand of hair. She had not forgiven him for what had happened last night. She had not forgiven herself, either.

"Feeding the colt. Go to bed." He shouldered past her and made his way through the living room.

Abbie followed, awake and indignant. "*You* go to bed. That's my horse. *I'll* take care of him."

He stalked to the porch, knelt beside Frosty and helped the colt to stand. Its long legs trembled, but Yates kept one hand under its belly to support it. The foal's ears pricked up, and it opened its mouth greedily for the bottle.

Abbie knelt beside him. "Give me that," she ordered, holding out her hand for the bottle.

He ignored her. "Go back to sleep."

"Did you feed him all last night? How did you do it without waking me? Haven't you slept?"

"The more I work, the sooner I get out of here."

She had been about to thank him, grudgingly, but his curtness irritated her. "Well, you can work even more and get out sooner if you leave my colt alone. Are you going to give me that bottle or do I have to take it?"

He gave her an eloquent sidelong glance. "I wouldn't try taking it if I were you."

The danger in his tone made her sit back on her heels, her muscles tensed, regarding him warily.

Despite the heater and the warmth flowing in from the living room, the porch was cold. Outside the blizzard still raged. She shivered. The porch windows were frosted thick with silver, and the wind keened and moaned, making the wood of the porch creak.

"Get inside," Yates said without emotion.

"I'd turn the heat up," she said, crossing her arms and hugging herself, "but the man who fills the propane tank was supposed to come today. He didn't make it. We've got to be running low. We're going to have to watch it."

He nodded.

"How much sleep have you had in the last two days?" she asked. "Three and a half hours? Is that all?"

He didn't answer. Through the fabric of his shirt, she could see his muscles bunch and rearrange themselves as he shifted to support the colt more firmly.

"I can be just as stubborn as you," she said. "Go ahead and feed him. I'll clean up this place."

She reached for the box of oversize garbage bags and shook one out. But when she rose and took up the old push broom and dustpan, she saw that he must have changed the straw at Frosty's last feeding.

She gave another sigh of exasperation, scooped what straw was soiled into the bag and tied it shut. Then she stood, her hands on her hips, staring down at him. "I don't know why you're doing this. Are you trying to be some kind of hero or something?''

Yates glanced up at her with narrowed eyes. He looked tired and on edge. ''Speaking of heroes,'' he said, ''what do you suppose the temperature is in Hawaii right now?''

Then he turned his attention back to the colt. His sarcasm, the contemptuous look on his face, made Abbie so angry she clenched her fists. ''You have no right to talk about poor Lucky—''

An odd look crossed Yates's face. Slowly he smiled, but the set of his mouth was bitter, almost cruel. ''That's right. So I won't. I'm tired. I forgot myself. Sorry. Damned sorry.''

Abbie frowned, puzzled. The scorn in his voice seemed tinged with regret. His mouth twisted in disdain, yet pain shone in its line, as well.

She studied his face, her own growing less angry and more somber. With a painful little pitch of her heart, she realized that as much as he could confuse and enrage her, she liked looking at him the way he was now, with Frosty. It was insane, but she did.

He knelt in the straw, one brown hand grasping the bottle, the other expertly keeping the wobbly white colt on its feet. The open shirt with its rolled-up sleeves flattered him, emphasizing the muscularity of his arms, shoulders and chest.

He no longer looked priggish to her, not in the least. The golden light of the porch glanced off his black hair and burnished his skin to a deeper bronze.

He seemed to exude not mildness, but power. It was eerie, as if fatigue unleashed something he'd kept hidden until now. There was gentleness, even kindness, in the way he handled the colt. Yet there was a forcefulness in him she hadn't seen before, and an aura of danger seemed to crackle around him.

Then, to her chagrin, she realized that he and she had locked gazes too long and that too much emotion, wanted or not, coursed between them. She remembered again the dreadful scene they had enacted last night, and was shamed and frightened by it. But still she could not look away.

"Why are you doing this?" she asked softly. She wasn't even sure what she meant. Why was he feeding the colt for her? Or why had he changed and become so hostile about Lucky? Or why did he stare at her the way he did?

He was silent for a moment, as if weighing her question carefully. "Somebody has to," he said at last.

She had the mysterious conviction that his answer, like her question, carried more than one meaning.

"Go back to sleep, Abbie." Great weariness seemed to weight his words. "Let's not fight. We're supposed to be partners. You help me. I help you. Remember?"

A pang of sympathy for him stabbed her, and reluctantly, she had to respect his endurance. "I've had more than enough sleep. I'm going to the barn to take care of the horses. Please be in bed when I get back. Get some sleep— please."

But Yates seemed dead set on staying awake. When she came out of the bedroom, her clothes changed, he had changed, too, and was wearing John's clothing again. He'd made a cup of instant coffee and was drinking it, standing up at the kitchen counter.

She tried to leave without him, but he followed, catching up with her. Darkness still obscured the sky, but the wind blew less sharply than yesterday, and the temperature had risen. Snow swirled down, but more slowly.

He caught her by the arm to let her know he was there. Even in the darkness, she could see the fatigue on his face. And he carried the box of wreaths, which she had forgotten.

"What are you doing *now?*" she demanded, shaking her head in despair.

The wind gave a sudden gust, and she staggered at its force. He tightened his grip on her arm. "I told you," he said, raising his voice to be heard above the storm, "we're partners. For as long as this blizzard holds."

Abbie lowered her head against the cold sweep of the snow, but she didn't shake off his hand. "You're impossible," she said. "Just impossible."

The wind rose in another unexpected blast that almost sent her reeling backward. Yates wrapped his arm around her and angled his body to keep her safe from the full force of the wind. He didn't look at her. He just kept pushing forward, keeping her at his side.

"Partners," he repeated grimly.

CHAPTER NINE

ABBIE'S MORNING blurred into a haze of impressions. The snowy cold and darkness of the outside world. The warmer pungency of the barn. The barn cats curled together to ward off cold. The horses stamping and snorting. Their white breath floating on the dark air when she turned them out, briefly, into the corral. Yates swinging an ax to break the ice in the water tank; its heater had broken during the night.

Abbie pitched straw and hay until her arms ached. Yates pitched twice as much as she. Mingus appeared, limping from the cold. He had tried to get the old pickup out of the shed, but the snow had drifted so deeply against the doors he had been shoveling for an hour and a half.

Yates went to help him. *How would we get anything done without him?* she wondered, standing by the door and watching his tall figure disappear into the snowy darkness. *How would I have gotten through all this without him?*

After what seemed a long, lonely time, he and Mingus returned to the barn to tell her that the storm had calmed just enough for them to take a load of hay to the nearest piece of range.

"If it stay like this," Mingus said, "I take a horse and the dogs, drive that one herd of cows down to the hay."

"I don't know," Abbie said dubiously. He could get lost if the blizzard rose again. But Mingus was adamant; he'd done it before, he could do it now.

"I'll go with you," Yates said, brushing the snow from his hat brim. There were holes in his gloves, and Abbie knew his hands must be half-frozen. She looked up at him with a mixture of sympathy and awe.

Mingus shook his head. "You just get in my way, boy. Two good dogs, I can do it."

Yates jutted his chin. "I know what I'm doing. I grew up doing this."

"You think so, boy?" Mingus said, a measuring gleam in his eyes. "I hear you're a city boy. You think you can handle this?" He nodded at the lowering sky.

Yates's jaw grew more obstinate. "Yeah," he said. "I think I can."

Abbie laid her hand on his arm. "No. Listen to Mingus—it's too dangerous. You're not used to it."

Yates gave her a look that was almost frightening. "You have no idea what I'm used to. None."

With a start, she realized he was right—there was much she didn't understand about him. She was finding him, in truth, a very mysterious man. But she still didn't want him to go. "You haven't had any rest."

His mouth took on an impatient crook. "Abbie, these are emergency conditions. Every man's got to do his part. I'm doing my part, all right?"

"But—"

Mingus nodded. "If he can help, I need him. Let him be, Abbie."

Embarrassed, Abbie drew her hand from Yates's sleeve. She held her breath. His face hardened again. "Don't worry about me. I'll be back as soon as I can. Take care of yourself, okay?"

An unexpected knot formed in her throat as she watched him leave a second time. She fought the desire to run after him, to make him take her gloves, but that was ridiculous because he wouldn't do it, and they wouldn't fit anyway.

She swallowed, trying to make the knot go away. It wouldn't.

She hung the wreaths, which looked incongruously cheerful in the morning's gloom. She petted the cats, who were cranky from the cold. Finally, she trudged through the snow back to the house, and when she opened the kitchen door, she heard a nicker from the porch. Frosty was awake and hungry again. One more task loomed before her.

It never quits, she thought. Resolutely, she added silently, *Well, that means I can't quit, either.* She prayed she could find the strength to feed him; he was growing more lively and rambunctious and would be hard to hold.

But this time feeding him was different. For the first time, Frosty stood by himself. His legs trembled, his ribs heaved in and out with the effort, and his feet didn't always go where he seemed to intend them. But he stood and walked a few tottering steps. He stayed standing even after he finished his bottle. He tried to sidle away when she gave him his shot. He snorted and tossed his head, his long legs quivering but gamely holding him upright.

Look at me, his dark eyes seemed to say. He flicked his tail and tossed his head. *Look at me—I'm really something.*

Abbie was so happy that she put her arms around his neck and hugged him long and hard. Her eyes stung with tears of gratitude that he had survived.

She hugged him more tightly. "You're going to make it," she told him, her voice broken with relief. "You will. Everything's going to be fine now. Just fine."

But she couldn't believe her own words, not yet. In a way, her devotion to the foal was like her love for Lucky—unfailing and true. But she wished she could stop thinking of the dark stranger out riding herd on her father's cattle in the snow.

Abbie soon saw that Frosty was going to be a bigger problem than ever. He tried to follow her into the living room, she had to build a makeshift barrier of dining room chairs and end tables to keep him on the porch.

It was time he was put with Jetta. Abbie was heartened but saddened at the same time. It seemed she had fought to almost the last drop of her heart's blood to keep this colt alive. Now that he no longer needed her to survive, she felt a pang.

But she celebrated his new soundness by taking a sinfully long shower. She dressed in clean pressed jeans and her favorite sweater, a powder blue one.

Then she went to the living room to call her father. She wondered why she hadn't heard from him. Perhaps he was on his way home even now. She would feel safer with him home again. Yates Connley was a far more complex and troubling man than she had reckoned.

She dialed the Hurleys' number and asked for her father.

"Abbie," he said, "I can't come home yet. The roads are drifted shut, especially those cuts along the seventeen."

"Oh," she said, disappointed. The seventeen was a seventeen-mile stretch of road that connected the Hurleys' ranch to SkyRim and the Bauer spread beyond. There it connected to the highway that led to Bison City.

"We're going out on the tractors in shifts. Me, Hurley, the Hurley boys. Carson, the foreman. The younger men started. They're due back soon. Then us geezers take over."

"Daddy, don't overdo it, all right?" She hesitated a moment. "Preston called last night. They're not coming home for Christmas. Marcie's mother has to have surgery. They're going there."

Frazier was silent a moment. "Well, too bad," was all he said.

Abbie hesitated again, then decided to bring things into the open. She was worried about her father, and she shouldn't be silent about it. "And there's something I didn't tell you. John told me about your blood pressure. Please don't work too hard. Promise me."

Frazier swore. He said John had a big mouth, and so did Preston for telling John. He asked why Preston didn't just hire a skywriter and spread the news all over the county. He said he was fine, fine, fine.

"Do you have your pills?" Abbie persisted. "Aren't you supposed to be taking pills?"

Frazier said yes, he had his blankety-blank pills, so there was no blankety-blank reason to worry.

Abbie restrained a smile. He certainly *sounded* healthy enough.

Frazier changed the subject. "How's Mingus? If this snow stays calmed down for a while, I want him to take a horse and the dogs and get those cows off the—"

"He's already gone. And Yates—the Connley man, I mean—went with him. He's not getting far with the computer. He keeps helping me—us—instead. You should tell him to stick to his own business. You're not paying him to muck out stalls and drive cattle."

"*Connley's* with Mingus? I'll be swoggled."

"You should tell him to stop."

"Stop? I've been over here all morning worrying about that herd and how you're getting on. Connley can handle himself all right, can he? Knows what he's doing?"

"He seems to. But he's trying to work two jobs at once, and you really ought to tell him—"

"Abbie, if he's man enough to pitch in, more power to him. At least *he's* not sitting on his miserable butt in Honolulu."

Stung, she gripped the receiver more tightly. "You promised you wouldn't criticize—"

"All right, all right," Frazier grumbled. "All I'm going to say is this—the best Christmas present you could get is to have that weasel drop out of your life."

"You *promised*," she said almost desperately. "How can we have a good Christmas if—"

"All right," Frazier said, more grumpily than before. "Forget I said a word. The Hurley boys are back. I've got to go. And Abbie . . ."

"Yes?"

"How's the colt?"

"He's fine. He's standing. I think he's ready to be with Jetta, if she'll take him."

"Glad to hear it," he said curtly. "'Bye, Ab. Take care."

He hung up. Abbie hung up, too, then stared at the phone pensively. She was moved that her father had bothered to ask about the colt. Even his terse comment, "Glad to hear it," meant a lot, coming from him.

She glanced out the window. The snow still fell slowly, the wind blew less shrilly. But the north was dark with new clouds rolling in, and she feared another, more vicious phase of the blizzard would soon be upon them.

THE LONGER Mingus and Yates were gone, the more concerned Abbie grew. The snow was starting to spin down more swiftly by early afternoon; the wind was rising, and the sky was darkening.

She tried to distract herself with her grandfather's computer. Yates said he had tried every possible word he could think of to access the disc, but perhaps she could find one that worked. After all, she had known her grandfather as well as anyone had.

For almost two hours she sat typing words on the keyboard. She tried every name that might have had significance to Old Mylo. Her grandmother's first name, middle name, maiden name. The names of Mylo's parents, his aunts, uncles, cousins, friends.

She tried the names of family dogs, of horses, of television personalities he had liked. She tried terminology from coin collecting, stamps, cattle ranching, Nebraska history, Nebraska place names.

Nothing worked. Every time she typed a word, the screen flickered the same message to her: BAD COMMAND. No wonder Yates had grown so sick of it. She steeled her determination and began to try names written backward: Mylo's, her father's, her own, the boys', all the dogs', even Oogly's.

Nothing worked.

But then she heard the stamp of feet on the back porch and forgot the computer. Her heart leapt with happy relief, for Yates was home.

She jumped up, ran to the kitchen and turned up the beef stew she had simmering on the stove. She'd defrosted a loaf of homemade bread and had it in the oven, ready to warm as soon as he arrived. He hadn't had either breakfast or lunch, and she'd insist he eat a hot meal, then go to bed.

She switched on the oven just as he came in the door, wiping his boots on the welcome mat.

Snow coated his Stetson, crusted his muffler, lined the creases of his jacket and caked his boots. He was stripping off the tattered gloves with difficulty, apparently unable to flex his fingers.

"Look at you," Abbie said in dismay, "you're half-frozen." Without thinking, she went to him, reaching up and untying the muffler. She hung it on a peg and began to brush the snow from his shoulders.

He gazed down at her, breathing hard, his eyes as dark as onyx. "Feel sorry for Mingus," he said. "He did this all day yesterday, too." He spoke as if talking hurt, and his face looked stiff with cold.

"Mingus is dressed for it," she answered. "All you've got are castoffs."

She helped him remove his jacket. He grimaced when he took off his ragged gloves. His hands were gray, and the knuckles of his right hand were scraped bloody. The blood had been frozen to the glove, and now the scrapes were torn raw again.

Abbie drew her breath. "Oh, Yates," she murmured unhappily, looking at his hands. "Do you still have feeling in them?"

"Too much."

"Come over to the sink, and soak them in warm water. I'll get the first-aid kit."

"It's no big deal," he muttered, but he hung up the Stetson and went to the sink. Abbie raced to the bathroom for the first-aid kit.

He was soaking his hands when she came back. He seemed to force a look of cheer to his face, but she could see how cold and tired he was.

"How are your hands?"

"Abbie, they're fine. No real damage done." He tore off a paper towel.

"Let me put antiseptic on those cuts," she said, seizing him by the elbow. "Come into the living room. Sit. Are your feet all right?"

"Everything's all right."

But, protesting, he let her lead him to the couch. She put the first-aid box on her lap, then ran her hand through her hair in confusion.

"No, wait," she said. "You should take a bath first. A long warm bath. That's what you do for frostbite."

"I'm not frostbitten. And I smell food. I'll eat, then take a bath. And why'd you build a barricade? Are the barbarians attacking?"

"No. Frosty is. He can walk."

"He can? I'll be damned. You did it, Abbie." He gave her a one-sided smile.

She tried to ignore the effect that crooked smile had on her heartbeat. "*We* did it. We're partners," she said, not meeting his eyes. "Give me your hand."

"Gladly." His voice made her heartbeat quicken even more, and she willed it to slow.

She took his hand, which was still cold, in hers. She tried to treat his scrapes with only scientific interest, but when she dabbed on the antiseptic, his fingers tightened around hers in reflex. Such a barely perceptible movement shouldn't affect her, but it did.

"I...don't suppose tape would stay in place there," she said, staring down at his hand in hers. She touched the injured knuckles gently, tentatively.

"No."

Abbie couldn't help herself; she put both hands around his. "You're still so cold," she said in concern. She wished that by sheer willpower she could infuse some of her warmth into him.

He was silent for a moment. "Is this how you treat your cowboy?" he asked quietly. "He's a fool to stay in Hawaii when he could come home to this."

Lucky. The name struck her like an arrow. She'd hardly thought of him in the past few hours—not since she'd talked to her father.

She tried to drop Yates's hand, but he would not release hers.

He looked into her eyes. "I've been thinking about last night. I thought about it out there on the range. In the snow. It kept me warm."

"Don't..." she protested, trying again to draw away.

He held her fast. "I'm not sorry it happened. But I don't want to hurt you. The trouble is, I don't want *anybody* to hurt you."

His hand, cold as it was, seemed to burn hers. She shook her head in confusion. "Don't talk this way. I told you—I love Lucky."

"No. You don't." He leaned nearer to her.

Abbie should have cringed away, but found herself paralyzed, incapable of moving away. She wanted to read the secrets in his eyes. She tried, but was powerless to do so, and it frightened her.

"Yes," she whispered. She *had* to love Lucky. Loving him was her identity. He was universally misunderstood, but she understood him. No one had ever loved him; she would love him and no one else for her whole lifetime.

Weariness mingled with torment in Yates's expression. "No," he said. She averted her face. With his free hand, he turned it back to him, raised her chin so that she had to look at him.

"No," he said again. "Abbie, you worked yourself to collapse to save a colt that nobody else would have bothered with. I think I know you. You were the kid that brought home every baby bird that ever fell out of a tree. You took in every stray dog, stray cat, no matter how sick or sorry. You've probably sat up nights with orphaned rabbits and God knows what else.''

"Stop—" She passionately denied what he said because it was so true.

She *had* taken in every fallen bird, every orphaned rabbit, squirrel and once, to her father's disgust, even a baby coyote.

She cared for all the rejected or orphaned foals or calves. She never turned away lost or abandoned cats and dogs. She fed them, ministered to them, found them homes.

If they were too deplorable for anyone else to take, she kept them herself. In the barn lived Morris, a fat yellow cat with three legs and only half a tail. Keeping Morris company was Murphy, a mud-colored female cat with one eye and lopped ears. And, of course, under the sun porch lived Oogly, a big, woolly lame dog that slunk away from everyone except Abbie.

"Abbie—" Yates leaned closer "—can't you tell? Won't you admit it? Lucky Gibbs is just another stray. You don't love him for what he's got, but for what he hasn't. You look at him, and all you see is need. You think he's one of the walking wounded. He's got you fooled.''

Abbie shook her head and once again tried to free her hand. Once again he held her fast. "You know *nothing* about him," she said. "You have no right—"

"I know more than you think. I do have the right. I thought about it a lot out there, Abbie, and I've got to—"

The ringing of the phone cut him off. He stopped, looking tired and disgusted with himself. He passed a hand over his eyes. "I don't even know what I'm doing," he muttered, his voice full of bitterness.

"Let go of me," she said with equal bitterness, jerking her hand away. She rose, her face burning, and made her way to the phone.

Her temples throbbed. She put her hand to her forehead.

"Hello," she said, grateful for the distraction, grateful to escape the things Yates was saying.

"Hi, Abnormal. It is I, your smartest, handsomest brother."

Abbie gave a shaky smile, recognizing Adon's voice. "Adon, when are you coming? I wish you were here now. John can't come home and neither can Preston. Tell the boys we've got a brand-new colt. They're going to *love* him."

Adon paused a moment. "I already talked to John and Pres. Listen, Abbie, I really wanted to be there. I wish I could be there. I wish we could all be there, because I think you're going to need us. But I can't—we can't."

Abbie couldn't comprehend. "Adon...you *can't?* What do you mean?"

She could hear the regret in his voice. That Adon, her most comic brother, sounded so serious, unnerved her. "Ab, Laurel and the kids and I went to her parents last weekend. You know, to have an early Christmas with her folks."

"Yes?" Abbie said, still not understanding. Adon and Laurel always handled the holidays this way. The weekend before Christmas at her parents. Christmas itself at SkyRim.

"We came home last night," Adon said with disgust. "While we were gone, a pipe broke in the upstairs bathroom. Water everywhere. It must have been pouring down since Friday night. Right into my office. Right onto my desk, dammit."

Abbie was dismayed to the point of tears. "The pipe broke? Your office flooded?"

"I never saw such a mess," he said, and she could tell he was shaken. "There's probably four hundred gallons of water in the carpet. My computer's shot. I've got to get another, install everything again. Laurel's stuff, too. All her teaching exercises. Her master's thesis."

"Oh, *Adon*," Abbie said, sharing his pain.

He swore. "The ceiling's about to cave in. I've got a crew of guys propping it up right now. The walls are ruined, too."

She could do nothing except repeat helplessly, "Oh, Adon. Oh..."

"Abbie, we can't leave it this way. We're going to have to stay and clean up the mess. I feel lousy about it, the kids are bawling their heads off, Laurel breaks into tears every time she even *thinks* of it—but we can't come. I'm sorry, we just can't."

Abbie felt stunned to numbness. Adon and Laurel and the boys weren't coming home for Christmas, either? Nobody was coming home? It was the last Christmas at SkyRim, the first without her grandfather, and *no one* was coming back to share the holiday?

She could say nothing. She kept her lips clamped tightly shut so they wouldn't tremble.

"Now, look, Abnormal," he said gruffly, "I really wanted to be there. I know we don't agree about SkyRim's being sold and all, but John said he told you about Dad. Do you understand now why we all agreed he should sell?"

"I understand," she said tightly.

"I don't want it to come between us."

"It won't," she promised, but she was having a difficult time not crying.

"The other reason I wanted to be with you is, well, because of Lucky. You know none of us like him."

"You don't *understand* him," Abbie objected in despair.

"Maybe you don't, either," Adon said cryptically.

"Adon, I told John I won't talk about this anymore."

"I think it's time we did."

"No! I mean it! Isn't it enough that none of you'll be here? Don't make it worse."

"Abbie, listen—"

"No!" she cried again. "Don't. Just don't."

"Abbie," he said, his voice taut, "I don't want you to hate me..."

"I could never hate you. I *love* you."

"Now, don't go getting emotional on me."

"Can't anybody in this family except me say, 'I love you'? What's wrong with us?"

"Abbie, I can tell you're getting really upset, and I don't want that. I'll call again later. Can I talk to Dad?"

"He's not here. He's out with the Hurleys, trying to clear the seventeen."

"Have him call when he gets home."

"Yes."

"And, Abbie...maybe none of us are good at saying it, but we all do... care for you, okay?"

She was crying now, and furious at herself for doing it. She brushed a tear away with self-disgust. "Okay."

"Oh, no. You're crying. I can tell. Look, everything is going to work out for the best. I mean that. I promise. Maybe it doesn't seem like it, but it will. I'll talk to you later. 'Bye."

She no longer knew what he was saying, or cared. "Goodbye," she said mechanically and hung up. She stood, stunned, staring down at the phone.

She felt Yates standing close behind her. "I heard," he said, his voice low. "I'm sorry."

She turned to him. She could see from the expression in his eyes that he wanted to take her into his arms again. Against her will, she half wished that he would. Furious with herself, she pushed the thought away.

Angrily, she swiped at her tears. "I'm taking Frosty to the barn," she said, not looking at Yates. "I'm getting out of here. I can't spend another minute in this house."

"I'll help you."

"I don't want your help," she retorted. "I'm sick of your help. Leave me alone."

"I'll carry him out for you. Then I'll leave you alone."

"Please see that you do."

"Abbie, I am sorry. About everything. I keep getting out of line. I'm not usually... I don't usually..."

"Don't say anything," she ordered, and felt herself dangerously near to tears again. So many emotions churned within her that if he took her into his arms, she would probably melt against him, grateful for the human comfort, grateful he was the way he was, wrong of her as that might be. Then she would truly hate herself.

But he did not try to touch her.

He stood looking down at her. "I'm sorry about all this," he said, then looked away.

OUT ON THE FROZEN RANGE on horseback, Yates had felt like a man knocked backward in time. The world hadn't seemed that elemental, that straightforward since he was seventeen. And on SkyRim's wide and snowy sweep of land, he had been crazy enough to convince himself that he could tell Abbie the truth.

Out there, things seemed both simple and true: he had come to help her, not hurt her. She had to see the truth.

She couldn't love Lucky Gibbs. She didn't even know the real Lucky Gibbs.

She was fooling herself because Gibbs played on her sympathy and pretended to offer her the sort of life she wanted. All she had to do was understand that, understand that she didn't love him, and then she wouldn't really be hurt.

Then Yates and she could sort things out, somehow. It all became hazy to him at that point. But he was sure he could be honest with her, and then they could be honest with each other, and then . . . hell, he didn't know what then.

But back at the house, nothing seemed either simple or true. She really *did* love Gibbs in her crazy softhearted way. And Yates couldn't tell her the truth. Too many bad things were happening to her.

She was going to be deeply hurt, and he was the instrument that would inflict that hurt. All he could do was give her a little time.

He would do what he had to, then leave her behind. Maybe someday he'd come back, see if she could forgive him. But, no. She couldn't. In her place, he wouldn't himself.

So he helped her take the colt to the barn.

He bundled a bewildered Frosty into an old quilt, and hoisted him up into his arms. The trek to the barn seemed longer and more arduous than ever before, the cold more punishing.

But, in spite of Abbie's worry that Jetta or her filly would reject Frosty, both seemed to accept him calmly. Jetta nosed the newcomer. She sniffed, snorted, then nosed him again. She stepped sideways, turning her flank nearer to him. Abbie petted the mare and talked baby talk to her.

Yates nudged the colt toward the mare's udder. Frosty stood trembling for a few seconds, then with unerring instinct, he stretched out his neck and began to nurse. He took a step nearer to the mare, switched his tail emphatically and gave himself over to the new pleasure.

The mare snorted, pawed gently at the straw and let him. Abbie praised her extravagantly, then fell into silence.

Yates found himself standing, staring across the mare's back at her. Their eyes met, and Yates saw the sadness and confusion in hers. He was the first to turn his gaze away. He pulled down the brim of his hat and stepped from the stall. "Well, I guess we can let nature take its course."

Abbie nodded.

He shifted his weight from one booted foot to the other. "I suppose you want to be alone now."

She nodded again.

She sat on a bale of hay and stared down into the mare's stall. He wished he could say something to comfort her. He knew he could not.

He turned and left her alone there. *Forget her,* he told himself savagely. *Just forget her. All your life you've been able to forget things, to pretend you feel nothing. Do it again, you damned fool.*

Always he had held his emotions in check. Now they rose up, struggling to be free, but he had no choice except to force them back more harshly than before.

The wind howled, the snow was thickening again, and the sky had darkened to almost nighttime darkness. Around him stretched the cold empty spaces of Nebraska, as if mocking the emptiness he felt inside.

CHAPTER TEN

ABBIE SAT for a long time in the barn, staring unseeingly into the middle distance. Something within her seemed to be dying. Perhaps it was the last trace of her childhood.

SkyRim would be sold soon. There was no helping it. She had wanted one final family Christmas at the ranch like old times. But there would never be another such Christmas. And last year, unbeknownst to them then, had been the last holiday they would ever have with Old Mylo.

This year, one by one, the boys had canceled, tied by their responsibilities to their own homes. Each of them now had another family, a new one that superceded the old.

Life was going on, and it could never be the same again. All she had left was Lucky and the dream that he and she together could preserve something of the old ways.

But her family distrusted Lucky; even Yates, a stranger, spoke against him. Abbie was so filled with tumult that at the moment she was afraid to admit that sometimes Lucky made her feel doubtful, too.

She would not tolerate the thought. Everything would work out with Lucky—but only if she, Abbie, were faithful and giving enough. She must never doubt the dream or she would destroy it.

Yates Connley, for no good reason, was trying to make her doubt. Doubt was dangerous, doubt was terrible. Abbie wanted the man gone from SkyRim. She wanted him gone as soon as possible.

She waited for what seemed a long time. She wanted to give Yates enough time to eat, shower, fall asleep. He *had* to fall asleep—he was so tired that even he admitted he hardly knew what he was doing.

At last she went back to the house. It was silent, and the elaborate Christmas ornaments seemed to mock her. She moved softly down the hall and opened the door to Adon's room to see if Yates was asleep.

Her heart gave a small painful lurch when she saw that he was. He was shirtless, the white sheet pulled halfway up to his chest. One muscled arm was flung wearily across the bed, almost as if reaching for her.

His dark hair looked blacker than usual against the whiteness of the pillow, his skin more bronzed. His chest was covered with a glistening fleece of ebony hair that made Abbie look away guiltily. His darkness still seemed exotic to her, more fascinating than she wished it to be.

She bit at her upper lip and pulled the door shut quietly. She would go to work in her grandfather's office again. If she could discover the code word that would open the computer disc Yates could do his inventory and be gone.

She went into the office and sat at the library table. She tried not to think of Christmas, or the boys, or of leaving SkyRim, or of Lucky's being so far away. Instead, she concentrated on discovering the disc's secret.

For almost five hours Abbie sat at the computer, stopping only to go into the kitchen from time to time to pour a cup of coffee.

Each time she failed to find the password, the more determined she became to succeed. After all, she told herself, setting her jaw, she'd been closer to Old Mylo than anyone. If anyone could guess his password, she was the one.

She would do it, and then Yates would be gone. No matter how tired or bored or frustrated she grew with the stubborn computer, that thought kept her going: find the password, and then Yates would be safely out of her life.

But at last, she leaned forward, crossing her arms on the table and hiding her face in them. Her eyes were closed, but the computer screen still seemed to shimmer before them. Phantom letters taunted her: BAD COMMAND, BAD COMMAND, BAD COMMAND.

Oh, she thought, it was useless. She would never find the password, her father would never come home, and she would be locked in this house with Yates forever. To guess the right word would be impossible. She had been a fool to try.

She squeezed her eyes shut more tightly. She remembered the fairy-tale princess who had the impossible task of discovering the name of an evil elf—or else she had to give him her child. The princess had been lucky, for her huntsman had discovered the elf dancing gleefully in the forest, singing that the child would soon be his, for nobody could ever guess his peculiar name: Rumpelstiltskin.

When the huntsman told the princess, she foiled the elf. He grew so angry that he spun round and round until he screwed himself right through the floor and disappeared forever.

The elf's angry spinning had always been Abbie's favorite part of the story, and she'd had her grandfather tell it again and again.

Her grandfather had told her the story of Rumpelstiltskin.

Abbie sat up with a start, blinking at the computer screen. *Her grandfather had told her again and again the story of that secret word.*

She shook her head. "Rumpelstiltskin" couldn't be the password. It was too long. Yates said the password could be no more than seven characters; it was a technical matter.

Still, Abbie had tried everything else. Dubiously, not daring to hope, she typed in the first seven letters of the name: RUMPELS. Then she hit the Enter key. She waited for the familiar clickety-click to precede the ever present reply of BAD COMMAND.

But this time the computer made a long soft whirring sound. Abbie watched the screen as if hypnotized, still waiting for BAD COMMAND to appear.

But instead, a series of numbers and letters flickered into life, filling the screen. A long list appeared as if by magic.

Abbie's excitement was so intense her stomach pitched. *The inventory! This list was the inventory that Yates wanted so badly!*

She stared at the columns, holding her breath. They were headed: HOLDINGS, PART ONE: COINS, Graded by Greenleaf Hologram Program. In the upper corner was the date—almost eighteen months ago, just before she'd met Lucky.

Beneath the heading, a subtitle read: Coins, American, Silver, 1779-1799, with Greenleaf Hologram Grading.

Abbie, her jaw set in concentration, paged down the computer entries. There it was—a list of all of the collection's holdings. She'd done it.

Eagerly she went to her grandfather's safe, dialed the numbers and started going through Mylo's "slab" albums, the albums that kept the coins safely encased in small slabs of plastic. It was the first time she'd touched the albums in over a year. They gave her a shiver of nostalgia for her grandfather.

His coding system for the albums was eccentric, but she soon found the album of American silver coins starting at 1779.

Eagerly, she went back to the computer. She could start checking the contents of the albums against the inventory. She couldn't appraise; only Yates could do that, but she could start confirming the inventory—it would be that much sooner he could be gone from SkyRim.

Abbie was elated at her success, yet an odd sense of emptiness haunted the edge of her consciousness. She thought of Yates's dark hair against the white pillowcase, his brown arm stretched toward her. She remembered the black sweep of his eyelashes against his cheekbones.

I want him gone, she told herself for the hundredth time. *I wish he was gone already.*

But soon she wished Yates was there, by her side. Her smooth brow furrowed in puzzlement. The coins in the album didn't match the inventory list. In fact, the inconsistencies were disturbing, extremely disturbing.

First, Mylo's best 1796 Myddelton token, the pride of his collection, was gone. The large silver coin had been in perfect condition—it was worth over $5,000. Mylo would *never* have sold it. Never.

Several other coins were gone, including a 1792 silver-centered cent. Although badly worn, it was still a valuable piece, and one of Mylo's favorites.

Six more of the most valuable coins were missing, and Abbie was concerned. Had he put them aside from the others because they were more valuable? And if so, where had he put them?

She was about to return to the safe to see if Mylo had stored the coins in another album when she made an even more startling discovery. In the back of the album, in a small yellow envelope, was another coin, loose, not slabbed.

Abbie opened the envelope and gasped. It held a coin she had seen in photographs, but never in reality: a 1794 Liberty silver dollar in nearly perfect condition.

Her heart began to beat crazily. Mylo could never have afforded this coin—it was impossible. A coin like this was worth two hundred thousand dollars. It was worth more than the rest of Mylo's collection put together.

Where could he have gotten it? How could he have gotten it? And why had the other coins disappeared? Nobody in his right mind would have traded this valuable coin for the missing ones. Something was wrong, *very* wrong.

Suddenly, with a sickly twinge, she remembered Yates's story of the Claridge ring. Had her grandfather been able to afford this coin because it was stolen?

Had he been unable to resist its lure and traded his other coins for it? Abbie felt ill at the thought. She loved her grandfather and didn't want to imagine him dealing in stolen goods. Of course he had not been himself at the end. . . .

She rose quickly and looked in the safe, hoping to find the missing coins in another album. But she was distracted by several rolls of coins—Lucky's.

She remembered Lucky's asking her to send the roll of buffalo nickels to him in Hawaii. She also remembered being surprised that he had coins in the safe. Almost without thinking, she took up the roll labeled Nickels and and stared at it. "Don't open it," he had said. He had said it twice: "Don't open it. Just send it."

The roll's paper wrapper was constructed so that she could see both the top and bottom coins. They were ordinary buffalo nickels, worn and unremarkable. The whole roll might be worth only fifteen or sixteen dollars. It was rather ridiculous for Lucky to have stored it in the safe, and she wondered why he had done so.

Lucky had always been interested in Mylo's coins. Deeply interested. Could he have been *too* interested?

Some perverse demon of suspicion made her open the roll. She hated herself for doing so, but she did, anyway. The coins poured into her hand. She began to shake.

The top and bottom coins were as they had seemed, common and in poor condition. But the other thirty-eight made her suck in her breath.

They were one of the rarest sorts of the coin, the famous three-legged buffalos—a misstrike at the mint had accidentally obliterated the animal's fourth leg. And the coins were in excellent condition—gleaming, unmarred. They must be worth at least ten thousand dollars.

This was no gift for a host's child. What was Lucky up to? And how had the coins come into his possession? He always claimed to have no money, so what was he doing with a small fortune in buffalo nickels?

She looked around the room wildly. Were the nickels stolen, too? Had Lucky bought them on some sort of black market? And why did he want them sent to Hawaii?

She was still shaking when she noticed Yates's glasses set carelessly on a bookshelf. His glasses, she thought dully. She hadn't seen him wear his glasses since . . . early yesterday.

Usually he wore them all the time, but today he hadn't had them on once. How had he functioned without them? She hadn't noticed their absence—until now. She set the nickels on the desk and reached for the glasses.

She held them up to eye level and looked through them. The lenses changed the appearance of nothing. They had no curvature at all. They were just plain glass.

He's been wearing glasses he doesn't need. He acts mild mannered and bland, but he isn't. He's not what he says he is. He's not what he pretends to be. Why?

A nauseating wave of intuition swept over her. Yates was some kind of investigator—an insurance investigator, perhaps. He'd suspected something was wrong with the collection. He had lied to her. So had her father.

And both of them believed whatever was wrong had something to do with Lucky. She knew it. She didn't understand how she knew it, but she did.

Her knees felt shaky, too insubstantial to hold her.

Then she looked up. Yates stood in the doorway. He wore his usual white shirt, dark slacks, impeccably knotted tie. But the expression on his face was taut, as if on guard for danger. She didn't know why he was up so soon, but he seemed able to thrive on little sleep, a quality she found eerie.

"Abbie?" he said, raising one eyebrow. "Why are you holding my glasses? Put them down."

Abbie gripped them more tightly. "Who are you?" she demanded. "*What* are you? Why did you come here?"

He shrugged one shoulder. Too casually, she thought. "I'm an appraiser. I came to appraise."

"There are things missing from the collection. And there are things in the safe that shouldn't be there. You *knew* it was going to be that way, didn't you?"

His brows knitted into a frown. "Abbie, what are you talking about? What's happened?"

She made a gesture of contempt at the computer. "I got into *that*," she almost spat. "Your precious disc."

"What?"

He moved to the table, looked at the computer screen. "My God," he breathed. He turned to her. "You did it," he said. "How?"

He tried to take her by the upper arms, to draw her nearer, but she slapped his hand away from her in fury. "I'll never tell you," she declared. And before he could stop her, she stepped to the computer and switched it off.

The information on the screen died into darkness. He couldn't get it back, she knew, without her. She had the password. He did not.

"Abbie," he said from between his teeth. He took another step toward her. Then he glanced down at the desk. He saw the 1794 silver dollar resting alone beside the slab album. He saw the spill of bright buffalo nickels.

He reached for the wrapper of the nickels. She tried to stop him, but he was too swift. He stared down at it. L.L.G., it said. Buffalo Nickels, 1938 D. He glanced at the coins again. It was too late to hide them. He could clearly see what they were and that Lucky's initials were on the wrapper.

"Have these been in the safe the whole time?" he asked with a smile so crooked it was close to a sneer. "My God he's been *that* arrogant? He's been keeping the rest of Claridge's stash *here?*"

Abbie said nothing. Anything she said would incriminate Lucky—or it would be a lie.

Yates's eyes held hers. His smile died. "I almost told you about him," he said. "I tried to tell you."

"Who are you?" she demanded again. "What do you want with us? And what are these?" She brandished the glasses. "Some stupid sort of disguise?"

"I wanted to tell you," he repeated, his face grim. " tried—"

"I *hate* you," she cried, and flung the glasses at his chest as hard as she could. They bounced off and hit the corner of the library table, shattering one lens. "I hate you. And my father let you come here, didn't he? He knew. They a knew—everybody knew but me. Is that why nobody's coming home? They can't face me? Because of the way they've plotted against poor Lucky—''

"He's not 'poor Lucky,'" Yates said savagely. "He's Claridge's Enforcer. He was a courier of stolen goods, and he made off with a couple of hundred thousand in hot coins. Nobody told you because nobody was sure—until now. Nobody plotted. They didn't want to alarm you."

"*Alarm* me?" she said, with all the sarcasm she could muster.

He stepped toward her again and took her by the shoulders. He would not let her twist away. His hands seemed to send electricity ripping through her, branding her flesh. "Listen to me. We *couldn't* tell you. You'd warn him. You'd think it was your...your damned duty or something."

"He hasn't done anything," Abbie protested, tears rising to her eyes. "You can't prove it. This can be explained, somehow, I know—"

"Abbie," he almost snarled, "there was a guy busted in Texas. He said he was getting coins from Lucky, and that Lucky claimed he was getting them from some old man in Nebraska. He said Lucky had other sources, too. We suspected he had part of the Claridge stash. I didn't think he'd be so cocky he'd hide it *here*, but he did. That dollar—" He nodded toward the 1794 silver dollar on the desk "—it's hot, it's *stolen*. I can tell you when and I can tell you where. Authorities have been praying it'd turn up. Now it has. I'm sorry it was here, and I'm sorry it's Lucky, but that's the way it is."

"No," she argued, fighting back the scalding tears. "No! I won't believe you."

"Everybody's tried to warn you," he said, his teeth clenched. He gripped her shoulders so hard it hurt.

"Everybody's *wrong*," she insisted, shaking her head. "And what's it to you? What's he ever done to you? Why can't you just leave us alone?"

"This," Yates hissed, tapping his hearing aid. "He did *this* to me. He took away my job. He might as well have taken away my life."

He grasped her shoulder and bent nearer to her, his dark eyes so intense they were almost frightening. "Can't you see, Abbie?" he demanded. "It's got to be Lucky. *He* was the Enforcer. He was the second man in Claridge's apartment that night—the one we didn't expect. He got me from behind. He's the one who shot at me. Everything points to it. I'm sorry, but there's too much evidence. He's not your brave, underprivileged cowboy, Abbie. He's a punk and a con man."

"No!" She wrenched away from him violently. He had to let her go or she would have hurt herself. He stood watching her, breathing hard.

"What are you—an FBI man?" she demanded bitterly.

"No. Just an undercover cop—till this happened." He touched the hearing aid again. "They used me because I knew coins and could deal with Claridge. I could talk the talk."

"I'm calling Lucky," she said, stepping toward the door. "There's an explanation for this. There has to be."

"No," Yates ordered. "You can't. From Hawaii he could get to anywhere." He moved to place himself between her and the door.

Abbie drew herself up as defiantly as possible. "You'll have to *kill* me to keep me from that phone," she said coldly. "I mean it." Her eyes flashed with warning.

"Abbie, don't. He could get away."

But oddly, he stayed where he was. He did not make another move to stop her. Half-faint with anger and dread, she made her way to the phone. Her fingers shook when she looked up the number for long-distance information. They shook even harder when she punched the numbers. Her voice was unsteady when she asked the operator for the number of the Fetterman ranch.

It seemed an eternity before she at last reached the ranch and a housekeeper said she would get Lucky to come to the phone. All that time, Yates simply stood in the doorway, watching her. His face was grim, his eyes unreadable.

"Sugar," Lucky said cheerfully. "What's up? I was just thinking of you. Sent those nickels yet? These people've been so nice I just wanted to do something for their kid, you know? This is a great place, hon. I'm gonna bring you here someday, if I can ever get a little money in the bank."

Abbie closed her eyes. Her head pounded. He was lying to her. Boldly, happily, shamelessly, he was lying. She felt sicker than before.

"Lucky, I looked at the nickels," she said. It seemed the only thing to do was be honest. He might lie. She could not.

"You what?" he asked, his voice going dead.

"I looked at them," she repeated, running her hand across her closed eyes. "And there's more. There's a man here, Lucky. He said he came to appraise the collection, but he—"

"What?" Lucky said, clearly horrified. "You father said he wasn't going to have it appraised until the ranch sold. He said he was going to wait. He *lied.* Why in hell is somebody snooping around now? Why didn't you tell me? Don't talk to this guy, Abbie. Get him out of there. Now. I don't care how you do it, just do it."

"It's too late," she said tightly. "Lucky, something's going on. There are coins gone from Grandpa's collection...."

"He gave me a few," he said smoothly. "For our future. It was supposed to be a surprise for you. He didn't want the rest of the family to know."

He lies so well, Abbie thought in despair. *He lies so smoothly. Why can't he stop lying? Has he always been like this? Why couldn't I see?*

"Listen," she said, plunging on relentlessly, "there are things in Grandpa's collection, and I don't know where they came from. There's a 1794 silver dollar."

"It's mine," Lucky said quickly. "It's just a fake, a curiosity, like. Send it along with the nickels. There are a couple of other things. Maybe you'd better send it all, so it doesn't get mixed up with your grandfather's stuff. I'll give you a list. Send it express. But first, get that guy out of the house."

"Lucky, he's talking about somebody named Claridge. And a shooting. And—"

"Baby, get him *out*. This is some dirty trick your father's trying to play—I know him. Get that stuff to me. Don't let anybody know—just do it. Hey, I've got an idea. As soon as I get everything, I'll cash in the good stuff and send for you. I could get a job on a ranch over here. How'd you like to get married in Hawaii, sugar? Live here, even? Just send the stuff."

"I'm sending nothing," she said, and then she could say no more. She pressed the button, and the line went dead. A sinister buzz droned in her ear. She listened to it for a moment, her heart hammering painfully. Then she hung up the phone.

Yates studied her face, his dark eyes so steady that she felt shakier than before.

His mouth took on its unhappy sneer again. "I suppose you thought you had to do that," he said. "That you owed him that much."

She raised her head, blinking hard. "I suppose I did. Yes. I owed him that much."

"Yeah," he said bitterly and looked away. "I figured you'd see it like that."

"I've got to get out of here," she muttered, fighting to maintain her self-control. "I'm going to check on Frosty. Don't try to come with me. Don't try to follow me. Just get out of here. I never want to see you again."

She stalked to the kitchen and began to bundle herself into her winter clothes. Yates stood in the living room, staring after her, his face stony. "Abbie, give me the password. Then I'll be out of here as soon as I can."

She had been winding her muffler around her neck. She stopped and let her eyes meet his. She could not tell him the password. Telling him would betray Lucky, something she had promised herself never to do, no matter what.

For a long trembling moment, she and Yates stared at each other. Her chest felt empty, as if her heart had dried up and fallen into dust.

Then she found herself saying, "Rumpelstiltskin is the password. Just the first seven letters." She spelled them, coldly and carefully. "Now," she said, "use it and get out. For once, I'd like to see a man keep his word."

Then she turned on her heel and left him standing there. She fled to the barn. She threw herself onto a bale of hay and cried until she cried herself to sleep.

Everything was gone now. Everything.

CHAPTER ELEVEN

IT WAS HER FATHER who woke her. "Abbie," he said. He had his arms around her. "Come inside. You'll freeze out here."

Abbie found herself leaning against his broad chest. Part of her wanted to fight him. Part of her wanted to rest there, loving him in spite of all that had happened. She could not leave his arms. She hid her face against his jacket.

"I'm sorry," Frazier said, awkwardly drawing her nearer. "About Lucky, I mean. We couldn't tell you. If it wasn't true—you'd never have forgiven us. And we couldn't have forgiven ourselves."

She kept her face hidden. She had searched her heart, and she knew what Frazier said was true. "I thought he was...different," she said, her voice dangerously near breaking. "I pretended he was different. Maybe I just wanted to be in love. So I pretended I was. And then I was too stubborn to back down. I don't know. Maybe I'll never know. I always was the stupid one."

"You're not stupid," Frazier said with passion. "You just let your heart lead you. It's a good courageous heart. It led you a little...astray, is all. Now don't cry. Are you going to get over that miserable cowboy?"

He drew back and gazed down at her with concern. She looked away, feeling guilty at her own blindness and stubbornness. "Everybody else saw what he was," she said miserably. "I wouldn't. Maybe it was to fight you. Maybe it was ... Oh, it doesn't matter. I was a fool."

"No," Frazier said, peering earnestly into her face. "You weren't a fool. You were fooled for a while, that's all. There's a big difference, Abbie."

"Is there?" she said bleakly.

"Yes. Everybody makes mistakes. I've made my share. Some with you. Maybe most with you. But none of us wanted to hurt you. None of us. The boys and I...well, we just flat didn't know what to do. They think the world of you. You know that."

"I know," she said, still not looking at him. "I see now what you meant about Lucky. Maybe I saw it long ago and didn't want to admit it. But I understand what you did. And I still love you all."

"Now, Abbie," Frazier said uncomfortably, "don't talk like that. You know I can't—I'm doing the best I can. Come back to the house. Connley's going. It didn't take much of a look at the inventory to prove what Lucky was up to."

Abbie stiffened. "I don't want to see him."

"Now, Ab," Frazier said, frowning, "don't blame him. The man was doing his job. Besides, he had a score to settle with Lucky. He feels...well, he doesn't feel good about what he had to do. Come on. Back to the house."

He tried to draw her to her feet. At last she let him do so, but she could not look him in the eye. "I warned Lucky," she said. "I shouldn't have. But I'd told him I loved him so many times I had to give him the chance to defend himself. I *had* to."

She swallowed. "But he couldn't. If he gets away, it's my fault."

Frazier kept his arm around her. He was silent for a moment. Then he said, "He didn't get away, Ab. Connley called Hawaiian authorities immediately. They got him—trying to board a plane to Samoa.''

She felt oddly unaffected by the news. It was as if Lucky Gibbs had never truly existed. He was a phantom only—a charming phantom she had once believed in. She had been foolishly bewitched by an illusion. She could never love the man he was.

''Oh,'' was all she said.

But she still didn't want to see Yates Connley. She turned away from her father. ''I don't want to go into the house while *he's* there,'' she said. Here, away from him, her emotions felt safely deadened.

''Now, Ab,'' Frazier admonished, ''he really is unhappy. But he had to do it.''

''Don't, please,'' Abbie said, going into the stall and kneeling beside Frosty. ''Just don't ask me to, Daddy. I've accepted everything else—selling SkyRim. That the boys can't come home. Even the truth about Lucky. All the things I thought I'd never accept. But I don't want to go back to the house while *he's* there. Don't ask me to do that. Give me that much, at least.''

''Ab, you can't stay out here. And if you were honest with yourself, you'd have to admit—''

''I've been as honest with myself as I can stand,'' she said with such vehemence that Frazier flinched slightly. ''Can't you let me have this one little thing? Please, just let me be until he's gone.''

Frazier sighed unhappily. At last he nodded. ''I suppose,'' he said, ''I can give you that much, at least. I'm sorry, Abbie.''

''I don't want anybody feeling sorry for me,'' she said, and meant it.

Frazier stood, gazing down at her. He acted as if he wished he could say something else. But he kept his silence. At last he turned and left her alone.

IT WAS LESS than an hour later when the barn door creaked open and Yates walked in, pulling it shut behind him.

Abbie had feared he might come, and she turned away from him. She had been refilling Jetta's feed trough, and she tried to ignore Yates and focus her attention on her task.

Yates walked to the stall and stood staring in, his face looking almost gaunt in the shadowy lamplight. He was dressed in his city overcoat and, under it, his suit, but his tie was untied for once, his shirt collar opened.

"I told you not to follow me out here," she said curtly, not looking at him. "I don't want to see you again."

"Who came to see *you?*" he said just as curtly. "I came for a last look at that swaybacked colt, is all."

"You've had your look. Now go away."

"No."

"Why?"

"Because I was lying again, dammit. I did come to see you. I have something to tell you."

"I don't want to hear it."

"I'll tell you anyway."

At last she gave him a glance, then wished she hadn't. His expression was almost forbidding and his stance dangerous with coiled power.

"What is it?" she asked with false interest. "How sweet revenge tastes now that you've got your man?"

"Somebody said once that revenge is the hollowest of emotions. I never believed it—till now. No, I'm not happy about any of this."

"That makes two of us."

"I *know* why you don't want to see me," he said.

"Do you? Then you know I've had enough men lying to me lately—for good reasons and bad," she said. "You're one more than I'm able to deal with, that's all."

"I'm the one you'd *better* deal with," he said with bitter emotion. "The same as I have to deal with you."

She gave him another scathing glance. "What's that supposed to mean?"

He took a step closer to her. He kept his hands in his pockets, but she felt somehow menaced by his coming nearer. "You've faced a lot since I've been here. You've accepted a lot. But there's one more fact to face."

Abbie gave a scornful laugh. "My, aren't you philosophical. Aren't you *wise.*"

"No. Not very. If you think you've been a fool, don't. I've been a bigger one than you'd ever hope to be. But I know one thing."

"Really?"

"You don't love Lucky Gibbs. You never did."

She raised her chin in contempt. "Don't tell me what I feel or don't feel."

"Yes, I will." He took another step closer. "You don't love him. He found you at a vulnerable point in your life. You fell in love with an *idea* about love—then you were afraid to give it up. You were afraid you wouldn't know who you are without him."

"Well," she said with irony, "I know now, don't I?"

"Do you?"

"Yes," she answered with a rebellious toss of her head. "I've been stupid, I've been stubborn, I've even been selfish and I've been blind . . . What do you want? For me to thank you for saving me from myself? That's a bit much, isn't it?''

"Maybe I've been stupid, stubborn, selfish and blind, too. A lot longer than you. Maybe I should thank you for saving me from myself. If I am saved. Am I? Can I ever be? Or is that too much, too?''

His words sent strange frissons dancing through the pit of her stomach. She stared at him in puzzlement and fought off an uncalled-for giddiness. *"What?"* she said.

He dropped his gaze to the colt, which slept, head curled to tail, in the straw. He shifted his weight and took a deep breath. "My father was like yours. Only more so. He never showed any feelings. Ever. When my mother died, all he did was tell me was not to cry. Men don't cry. When I went to live with my grandparents, I should have loved them. I should have loved that life. But real men didn't have feelings like that—or so I thought.''

Abbie watched with bewilderment as conflicting emotions played across his strong face.

"See,'' he said from between his teeth, "I just understood that I was supposed to be like him. But now I think that maybe something in him was...broken. Maybe the war did it, or police work, or my mother's death, I don't know. I just tried to be the same, that's all. I succeeded. Too well.''

Abbie felt a rush of compassion for him. "I—I don't know what to say....''

"Neither do I, obviously. Except that being here with you made me realize what I'd turned my back on so long ago. That I'd loved it and never knew it. I'd never turned around and looked back. Until now.''

Abbie shook her head helplessly. "I still don't understand."

He started to move toward her, but seemed to stop himself by an act of great will. "Abbie, maybe it's time that some man said to you what you've said to everybody except me."

He raised his eyes to hers again. "I love you," he said simply.

She gazed at him as if hypnotized. Her heart contracted so tightly it hurt.

He took his hands out of his pockets and made a futile gesture. "It's too soon to say it—it's wrong to say it, and it's selfish to say it—but I wanted you to know."

She shook her head as if to deny his words.

"No," he said, his face stormier than before. "I wanted you to know that if I looked at you as if I wanted you, or spoke to you as if I wanted you, it was true. I didn't do it to get information out of you or anything like that. What I said to you was often false. But what I felt for you was real. Maybe the most real thing I ever let happen."

Abbie's throat was tight with emotion. Lucky had said hundreds of pretty things to her—thousands—but the words always came easily to him. No one had ever said anything to her that seemed to be spoken at such great emotional cost.

He squared his jaw. "It was Lucky Gibbs who was the fool, not you. I mean it. He was, Abbie. Because if it had been me that you loved, instead of him, I never would have failed you. I would have died first."

Touched by his words to the point she could not speak, she took a step toward him.

"Don't," he said fiercely. "Unless you want to be in my arms, Abbie. Don't come any nearer. Unless you want it, too."

She stood, gazing at him in confusion and swept by tides of emotion she barely recognized. It was, of course, impossible to go to him. After all that had happened, after all her protestations of love for Lucky, she could not take that step toward Yates Connley.

But she did. Tentatively, almost reluctantly, she moved closer to him.

"Abbie?" he said, a world of questions within that one questioning word.

Still she could not speak. So she bit her lip, held his gaze and nodded.

He swept her into his arms and held her fast, speaking against her hair. "Abbie, Abbie. I think I loved you the minute I saw you. Let me hold you, just hold you."

But before either of them knew what was happening, he was kissing her so hungrily and passionately that Abbie felt as if he was drawing her soul out of her body. She kissed him back just as fervently. She wound her arms around his neck. She clung to him, knowing what she felt for this man was love, real love.

At last he broke off the kiss, breathing hard, and simply held her, crushing her against him. "I didn't want to admit it. But when I let you call him, let you warn him, I knew I loved you. I had to let you do it—if it was what you had to do. I couldn't hurt you anymore. Even if he got away. Revenge wasn't important. Even justice wasn't. Only you."

She nuzzled her face against his warm throat. "I *couldn't* admit how you made me feel. I didn't want to

admit it. But I gave you the password. That's the momen
I knew I didn't love him. Yet it didn't seem possible that
could have fallen in love with you."

"But you did?" he asked between kisses on her fore
head, her temple.

"Yes. Yes."

"But I lied. Just like he did."

"You couldn't lie about what you really were. You wer
strong and kind and dependable and deep...."

"Deep?" He laughed, hugging her tighter. "Me?"

"Yes," she said, drawing back so she could look up a
him. "Don't you even know it? You're *very* deep."

"Not me."

"Yes, you," she said firmly.

He kissed her long and tenderly. Abbie's soul shivered.

"I've got money in the bank," he said against her lips.

"I don't want to hear about your money."

"I won't buy the lousy security company. Who wants
security company? Who wants to play golf? Jog?"

"I don't want to hear about golf or jogging."

"I mean it," he said, drawing back so he could stare inte
her eyes. "I'll buy us a ranch. Maybe I'll buy *this ranch*
What would your father say to that?"

Abbie's lips parted in disbelief. "A ranch? This ranch"
SkyRim?"

"Why not? You're happy here. I could be happy here
I'm a physical guy, Abbie. I wasn't meant to sit behind
desk or keep track of business shares, or stroll around
golf course. I grew up doing this. I *liked* doing this. I stil
do—that's one of the things I found out here. So why can'
we do it together?"

"Oh, Yates," she said, tears rising in her eyes. "You'd do that for me?"

"I'd do anything for you. Merry Christmas, Abbie."

And he kissed her again.

Frosty lifted his head and nickered softly, as if irritated that the sanctity of his stall—and his sleep—was being violated.

But for once, Abbie ignored him. The world that had seemed so wrong was right again, blissfully right. What was hurt was well, and what was broken, healed.

She gave herself so happily to Yates's embrace that her heart seemed to soar and become one with the wide great Nebraska sky.

Let
HARLEQUIN ROMANCE®
take you

BACK TO THE

Come to the Diamond B Ranch,
near Fawn Creek, Arizona.

Meet Seth Brody, rancher. *And* Janna Whitley, city girl.
He's one man who's hard to impress. And she's a woman
with a lot to prove.

Read THE TENDERFOOT by Patricia Knoll,
January's hilarious Back to the Ranch title!

Available wherever Harlequin books are sold.

Make Christmas a truly
Romantic experience—with

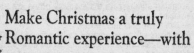 HARLEQUIN ROMANCE®

Wouldn't *you* love to kiss a tall, dark
Texan under the mistletoe? Gwen does
in HOME FOR CHRISTMAS by
Ellen James. Share the experience!

Wouldn't *you* love to kiss a sexy
New Englander on a snowy Christmas
morning? Angela does, in Shannon
Waverly's CHRISTMAS ANGEL.
Share the experience!

Look for both of these Christmas
Romance titles, available in December
wherever Harlequin Books are sold.

(And don't forget that Romance novels
make great gifts! Easy to buy, easy to
wrap and just the right size for a
stocking stuffer. And they make a
wonderful treat when you need a break
from Christmas shopping, Christmas
wrapping and stuffing stockings!)

©DG 1990   HRX

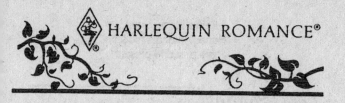

HARLEQUIN ROMANCE®

WELCOME BACK, MARGARET WAY!

After an absence of five years, Margaret Way—one of our most popular authors ever—returns to Romance!

Start the New Year with the excitement and passion of

ONE FATEFUL SUMMER
A brand-new Romance from Margaret Way

Available in January wherever Harlequin Books are sold.

Relive the romance...
Harlequin and Silhouette
are proud to present

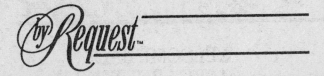
by Request™

A program of collections of three complete novels by the most-requested authors with the most-requested themes. Be sure to look for one volume each month with three complete novels by top-name authors.

In September: **BAD BOYS**
Dixie Browning
Ann Major
Ginna Gray

No heart is safe when these hot-blooded hunks are in town!

In October: **DREAMSCAPE**
Jayne Ann Krentz
Anne Stuart
Bobby Hutchinson

Something's happening! But is it love or magic?

In December: **SOLUTION: MARRIAGE**
Debbie Macomber
Annette Broadrick
Heather Graham Pozzessere

Marriages in name only have a way of leading to love....

Available at your favorite retail outlet.

REQ-G2

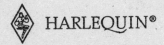
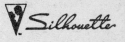

When the only time you have for yourself is...

TM

Christmas is such a busy time—with shopping, decorating, writing cards, trimming trees, wrapping gifts....

When you do have a few *stolen moments* to call your own, treat yourself to a brand-new *short* novel. Relax with one of our Stocking Stuffers—or with all six!

Each STOLEN MOMENTS title is a complete and original contemporary romance that's the perfect length for the busy woman of the nineties! Especially at Christmas...

And they make perfect **stocking stuffers**, too! (For your mother, grandmother, daughters, friends, co-workers, neighbors, aunts, cousins—all the other women in your life!)

Look for the STOLEN MOMENTS display in December

STOCKING STUFFERS:

HIS MISTRESS Carrie Alexander
DANIEL'S DECEPTION Marie DeWitt
SNOW ANGEL Isolde Evans
THE FAMILY MAN Danielle Kelly
THE LONE WOLF Ellen Rogers
MONTANA CHRISTMAS Lynn Russell

HSM2

 **WORLDWIDE LIBRARY** ®

Harlequin Romance invites you...

BACK TO THE

As you enjoy your Harlequin Romance® BACK TO THE
RANCH stories each month, you can collect four proofs of
purchase to redeem for an attractive gold-toned charm bracelet
complete with five Western-themed charms. The bracelet will
make a unique addition to your jewelry collection or a
distinctive gift for that special someone.

One proof of purchase can be found in the back pages of each
BACK TO THE RANCH title...one every month until
May 1994.

BACK TO THE RANCH	NAME: _____
	ADDRESS: _____
	_____
	_____
	CITY: _____
	STATE/PROVINCE: _____
	ZIP/POSTAL CODE: _____
	ONE PROOF OF PURCHASE 089 KAX

089 KAX